She wouldn't trade t

Bree looked over and saw that Charlie was ~~staring~~ staring. His eyes never leaving her, never wavering.

She was acutely aware that he could have glanced down to the tops of her pushed-up breasts, to her barely covered thighs. If he had he would have noticed the intermittent tremors, the pink skin she felt sure was not just on her cheeks but the tips of her ears.

It was unbearably sexy, that stare, his dark eyes so large, unblinking. As if he could see more than his share, more than she wanted him to.

As every second ticked by, the heat intensified, until she couldn't take it any longer.

"I want to take your dress off slowly. Let it fall down your body," Charlie finally said, his voice—still low and rumbly—moving through her like distant thunder. "I've been wondering for hours what's underneath...."

Blaze

Dear Reader,

My first true love is New York City. It sounds crazy, but I've been mad for Manhattan since the first time I went there as a kid. My father's from New York, so we'd fly out from California regularly. Later on, I had friends who were commuters, spending half their time in New York and the other half in L.A. I visited at least once a year, and knew my way around like a native.

So, when I came up with the concept for It's Trading Men! (why didn't they have this when I was younger?) I knew it was a New York tale. Ask any single woman who lives and works in the city, and she'll weep as she explains how difficult it is to find the right man in all the hustle and bustle of skyscrapers and subways.

Heroine Bree Kingston is a sweet girl from a tiny town in Ohio who had the guts and gumption to go solo into Manhattan to find her dreams. She never imagined she'd one day end up in the bed of Charlie Winslow, the blogging king of Manhattan, but that's where she finds herself, during Fashion Week, no less! But chemistry this sizzling and a match this perfect were way too good to last, right?

I hope you enjoy the fantasy and fun of *Choose Me*. Look for more It's Trading Men! stories with *Have Me* in March 2012 and *Want Me* in April 2012.

I love hearing from readers and can be reached at joleigh@joleigh.com. And come visit www.blazeauthors.com.

Happy reading,

Jo Leigh

Jo Leigh

CHOOSE ME

TORONTO NEW YORK LONDON
AMSTERDAM PARIS SYDNEY HAMBURG
STOCKHOLM ATHENS TOKYO MILAN MADRID
PRAGUE WARSAW BUDAPEST AUCKLAND

Recycling programs
for this product may
not exist in your area.

ISBN-13: 978-0-373-79669-4

CHOOSE ME

ABOUT THE AUTHOR

Jo Leigh is from Los Angeles and always thought she'd end up living in Manhattan. So how did she end up in Utah, in a tiny town with a terrible internet connection, being bossed around by a house full of rescued cats and dogs? What the heck, she says, predictability is boring. Jo has written more than forty novels for Harlequin Books. She can be contacted at joleigh@joleigh.com.

Books by Jo Leigh

HARLEQUIN BLAZE

To get the inside scoop on Harlequin Blaze and its talented writers, be sure to check out blazeauthors.com.

To Birgit, for her enthusiasm and support.
And to Debbi & Jill, who rock. Hard.

1

Bree Kingston
Assistant copywriter at *BBDA Manhattan*
Studied Advertising and Fashion at *Case Western University*
Lives in *Manhattan* ❤ Single From *Ohio*
Born on March 22

BREE KINGSTON HAD BEEN IN Manhattan for five months and twelve days. This was her third visit to the St. Mark's Church basement kitchen, where she and sixteen women she barely knew were exchanging ten days' worth of frozen lunches. She'd gotten invited by Lucy Prince, whom Bree had known for four days. Lucy wasn't part of the exchange. Not anymore. She'd moved to Buffalo with her fiancé, thereby freeing up the foldout ottoman bed that Bree slept on in the one-bedroom apartment she shared with three other girls. Bree's rent was a steal at seven hundred per month. The stove at the apartment had been nonfunctioning for as long as anyone there could remember.

Technically, this was her sixth visit to the kitchen.

She had gotten permission to come to the communal church basement the evenings before the exchanges to prepare her lunches. Sixteen portions of veggie lasagna and medium-heat chili this week packed in small freezer-to-microwave containers, all ready to be handed out during the semimonthly trade.

Although it had sounded odd when she'd first heard about the group, Bree suffered from both of the two major maladies that came with living the Manhattan dream: no decent single men to date and no money.

She'd anticipated both. Since she'd spent most of her twenty-five years planning her escape to The Big Apple, she'd read every article, blog and book about the subject, saved her money like Scrooge as she'd worked her way through college, and even had a decent savings account set aside for emergencies. Bree was in this for the long haul.

Finding the lunch exchange had been a brilliant stroke of luck. Fourteen of the sixteen were also single, worked in the East Village and all of them knew where to find the best happy hours, the cheapest dry cleaning, cell service that actually worked and where not to go on a date, assuming one ever had a date.

Even better, she'd actually made her first real New York friends.

"Attention ladies!" Shannon Fitzgerald, a natural redhead wearing a fantastic knockoff dress Bree had noticed first thing, had needed to shout to get everyone to listen. All of them were standing around a rectangle of tables, their lunches in front of them in neat little stacks. Everyone had brought their own cooler bag with ice packs on the bottom. In a moment, they'd move from pile to pile, an elegant assembly line of working women, all of them under thirty-ish, all of them

wearing something dark on this December day. All of
them except Bree. She had chosen a yellow-and-black
plaid skirt and jacket, emphasis on the yellow, hand-
made from her own copycat pattern. Which would have
looked very nice on Shannon, now that Bree thought
about it.

"Hush," Shannon said, and in a moment, the room
fell silent. "Thank you. I have had an idea," she said.

It wasn't just a sentence. Not the way it was said. No,
all the words were IN CAPS and **bold**, like a headline.
The **IDEA** was going to be good. Exciting. Way more
than just a new frozen lunch recipe.

"For those of you who are new—" Shannon nodded
toward Bree "—my family owns a printing press.
Fitzgerald & Sons on 10th Avenue and North 50th."

Bree had seen the place. It was huge.

"We do trading cards. Mostly sports, but now everybody and their uncle wants them. Artists use them as
calling cards, Realtors do the same. They've got them
for *Twilight, Harry Potter, The Hunger Games,* and
we just finished a ginormous order of official Hip-Hop
trading cards."

Shannon paused, looking around the room. Then she
smiled. "No one, however, is using trading cards the
way they *should* be used—*to trade men.*"

Bree blinked, shot a look at her closest friend, Rebecca Thorpe, only to find Rebecca staring back. They
raised eyebrows at each other and Bree was grateful
all over again that she and Rebecca had clicked at that
very first lunch exchange, despite their obvious differ-
ences. Bree was from a little town in Ohio and had a
huge middle-class family. Rebecca was an attorney, the
only child of a snooty New York family and she ran a
charity foundation, one of the biggest in the world. Still,

within five minutes of meeting, they'd made plans, exchanged digits and by that night they'd been friends on Facebook and LinkedIn and had already talked on the phone for over an hour.

"Intriguing," someone said, and Bree snapped back to the **IDEA** and the drama.

Someone else said, "Go on."

Shannon obliged. "Three weeks ago, I went out on a fix up. My cousin knew this guy who worked with this other guy, and you know the drill. He was great. Really. We met at Monterone—I know, risotto to die for—anyway, he was good-looking, his job was legit, he'd been with someone, but they'd broken up months ago. It was a really nice blind date, one of the best I've been on in ages. But *it* wasn't there." The redhead sighed. "Zero chemistry. I knew it, he knew it. However," she said, only it was **HOWEVER**, "I knew, straightaway, that he and Janice would hit it off like gangbusters."

Every eye turned to Janice. Bree had met her, of course, but she was one of the few Bree hadn't had drinks with. She was a cutie, too. Tall, brunette, great touch with makeup.

Janice grinned. "We've been out three times, and he's fantastic. I can't even believe it." Janice put her hands on the table in front of her and leaned over her frozen chicken enchiladas. "I'm going to meet his mother on Friday."

The whole room said, "Ohhh," in the same key.

"I know," Janice said, standing up again. Back straight, face glowing. As if she'd won not just the spelling bee but aced the math final, as well.

Shannon spoke. "We've all got them, you know. Men who are nice and cute and have steady jobs. Who aren't gay or taken or married and not telling. Combine that with my family's printing press and what you get is…"

This was like a Broadway show, Bree thought. Or the Home Shopping Network. She held her breath, waiting for the reveal, the **IDEA** in all its glory.

Shannon raised her hands. Holding in each one, a card. A beautiful, glossy card. A trading card fit for a Heisman trophy winner, for a Hall of Famer. "On the front," she said, "the picture. Of course." Then she flipped her hands around. "On the back are the important details. The stats that matter."

"Like…" Bree said, surprised she'd spoken aloud.

"First and foremost," Shannon said, "marry, date or one-night stand."

The women nodded. Hugely important. How much pain in life could be eliminated by knowing who was whom. Each had their place. Bree would never be interested in a marry. Probably not a date, although that would depend. But a one-night stand? God, yes. Someone prescreened? It would be perfection. A Manhattan girl's idea of heaven.

"His favorite restaurant," Shannon added, and again, there was a collective "Uh-huh." "Because while I'm a gal who likes the pub down the street, some of you might prefer a little Nobu action. Then there's his passion."

Silence followed this statement, but Shannon milked it, in no rush to explain, though even she had her limits. "You know as well as I do that all of them want to talk about themselves, and usually they want to talk about their thing. No, not *that* thing. I mean, their other main preoccupation. You know, the Yankees, or the stock market, or the iPad or foreign films. If you're into the Mets, you don't want to get stuck with a day trader. Or maybe you do, but, at least, you'll know going in. And finally," she said, taking yet another dramatic pause. "The bottom line. Full disclosure. Snoring might not bother me, but it might bother you. Chemistry is downright fickle. But we all deserve to hear the unmitigated truth. Google can only give you so much, am I right?"

Again, there was silence, but not because anyone was confused. The beauty of the **IDEA** was sinking in, was gelling, was blooming like a rose in winter. As one, the semimonthly St. Mark's frozen lunch exchange began to applaud.

Hot Guys New York Trading Cards was born.

WITH A QUICK GLANCE OUT the window at the snowplow spitting down West 72nd Street, Charlie Winslow pushed his chair across his office to computer number three, the Mac. There were six altogether, each running a different operating system, each rotating views of his *Naked New York* media group. There were setups like this, well not exactly like this, but similar enough, in an apartment in Queens, a bungalow in Los Angeles, a flat in London and an office in Sydney. Then there was the huge old mansion in Delaware where the bulk of his servers were housed.

Naked New York was a gluttonous bitch, needing constant attention. What had begun as a single blog about Manhattan in 2005 had become ten separate blogs generating at last count over two-hundred-million page hits per year, and far more importantly, roughly thirty million per annum in advertising revenue. *NNY* was just like any other conglomerate, only the products manufactured were ideas and opinions, words and tips, photographs and gossip. Ever changing to remain ever pertinent. The revenue stream was one hundred percent advertising, and while Charlie paid a small team of full-time employees and a very large team of contributors, each blog was his baby whether it focused on celebrities, finance, sports, technology, gaming or even the female perspective on life. He trusted his editors, but it was his name on every masthead.

Which had made Charlie a celebrity, at least in the important cities. He liked that part. Hadn't considered it when he wrote up the initial business plan, but there were worse things than getting invited to every major event and having stunning women eager to accompany him to each one. He wasn't in Clooney's league, but Charlie's determination to remain a bachelor had passed from joke to fact to legend in the span of six years.

His phone rang, a call, not a text, and he answered, his Bluetooth gear attached to his ear directly after his morning shower. "Naomi. How are you today, gorgeous?"

"Filled with wonder and delight, as usual," his assistant said, her voice a nasal Brooklynese, her tone as dry as extra brut champagne.

Charlie grinned. "Any changes?"

"Nope. Just don't forget that the tailor is coming by at eleven. Don't make him wait. You did last time, and while you're precious as diamonds to me, his client list would make you tremble."

"You're always so good for my ego." Charlie glanced at his handset to see who wanted to interrupt his call. It was his cousin Rebecca. Odd, she rarely texted on a workday. "Got to run."

Naomi hung up even before Charlie pulled out the phone's keypad.

What's wrong? Has someone died? CW

A moment later, his phone beeped as his screen refreshed.

Everything's fine. I have a treat for you, though.

He sailed across his floor again, this time to check the stats on one of his latest clients. Their ads had been on rotation in five markets, and they were doing well in four.

What kind of treat? CW

A date.

He laughed. His thumbs flew.

Come on, Becca. CW

She was his favorite cousin, which was saying something because he had a ton of them. His parents each had five siblings and they'd all bred like rabbits. Charlie had three siblings of his own, but only one had climbed aboard the baby wagon.

Instead of the beep announcing a return text, his phone rang. Charlie switched to voice.

"Seriously," Rebecca said. "I think you'll get a kick out of her. She's…different. She's new. Brand-new. Still, wears colors, for God's sake. And she's bright, tiny, funny and completely starstruck. She'll swoon over you, and make that head of yours so large you won't be able to fit through your front door."

"Ah, Rebecca. I didn't know you cared. She sounds perfect."

"I'm betting you're not booked for Valentine's day."

He sighed. "Don't be silly. I never plan that far in advance."

"You will this time."

He looked away from his monitor at the sound of her voice. Teasing, as always, but he hadn't missed the dare. He liked a challenge, and Rebecca was clever. Really clever. "Fine."

"I'll be in touch."

"What's her name?"

"Does it matter?"

He inhaled as his hands went to his keyboard. "Nope." Charlie clicked off and two minutes later, he was lost in a conference call, Valentine's Day and intriguing puzzles forgotten.

Bree had made chickpea veg curry and mac and cheese for her frozen meals, but like everyone else in the big kitchen, she wasn't here for the food.

Today was CARD DAY.

The past few lunch exchange meetings had been more focused on the trading cards than food. Everyone, with one notable exception, had offered up at least two men to the trading card list. They'd brought in pictures, supplied the back copy, agreed that *all* first dates were to be held in very public venues, with the submitter knowing the details and phone numbers involved. Then, Shannon had done mock-ups of the cards, changed them twice until they had a design that worked. The actual printing of the cards hadn't taken that long, but time had stretched like putty since that day in December. Finally, a month and a half later, here it was. There was actually a chance, remote as it might be, that Bree would find a card that had her dream man on the cover, and all he'd want was a night that would blow the lid off this town.

She didn't deserve to find Mr. Right Now, though. Because Bree had brought zero men to the table. Zilch. Nada. She knew some single men at the advertising agency, but she'd never gone out with any of them. Not that she hadn't been asked. But she was planning on moving up in the company as quickly as possible, and didn't want to make any alliances until she'd been there at least a year. She might be from Ohio, but she hadn't just fallen off the turnip truck.

Bree had plans. More specifically, she had a five-year plan. End goal: to become a fashion consultant, author and television personality. The plan was her guiding light, her pathway through the Manhattan madness. One cornerstone of the plan was that under no circumstances was she to get involved with a man. Yes, a girl had needs. She'd been on dates since she'd moved to New York, but only a couple of them had included sex. The earth hadn't moved either time, which meant that the idea of a selection of eligible, vetted, one-night men hadn't been far from her thoughts since December.

Scary thing, being mostly friendless in a city like Manhattan. Thrilling, too. But the men were different than the ones she'd known back home. The rules here seemed to be more…fluid. The stakes higher.

Thank goodness her friendless status had changed as a result of the lunch exchange. Enough, in fact, for her to have been included in the trading card deal even when she hadn't contributed.

Shannon entered the room, and chaos ensued. Frozen meals were abandoned without a backward glance as the women huddled around one empty table. Shannon's penchant for drama made her lift her cardboard box high in the air only to tip it over, covering the table in a cascade of beautiful, practical possibilities, all on 2.5 x 3.5 thick-coated stock, suitable for purse or wallet, as a handy reference, as a focal point for dreams and wishes.

Bree's gaze swept over the puddle of cards, her eyes wide, adrenaline pumping, hoping for someone nice, but not too nice. Someone easy.

Rebecca came up next to her and bumped into her shoulder. Bree glanced at her friend, but only to scowl. When she looked back down at the cards, her breath stilled and for a moment, her heart did, too. There was a single card away from the pile, directly in front of Bree. On it was a picture that sent Bree's heart racing.

It couldn't be. Not possible. The sounds of her friends dimmed behind the whoosh of blood in her ears as she reached with trembling fingers to pick up the card.

Charlie Winslow. *The* Charlie Winslow. It had to be a joke, a trick. He could have anyone. He'd already had practically everyone. Why would he be on offer in the basement at St. Mark's Church?

"I thought you might recognize him."

Bree tore her gaze from the card to look once more at Rebecca. Her friend's smile was as smug as if she'd gotten past the velvet rope at The Pink Elephant, but Bree couldn't hold out for long. She stared again at the trading card, double-checked. Still Charlie Winslow. "How?"

"He's my cousin," Rebecca said.

"Your cousin," Bree repeated.

"Yep. God knows he's single."

"He can have anyone."

Rebecca chuckled. "Yeah, but if all you're eating is

lobster and champagne every night, it's bound to get boring, don't you think?"

Bree shook her head. "Not even a little bit. Although now I understand why you're part of the lunch exchange. We're the tuna fish to your normal caviar, am I right?"

Rebecca dismissed the deduction with a roll of her eyes. "Trust me. He's bored. And he needs a date for Valentine's night."

Bree took a step back, just to keep her balance. "Me? I'm…" She blinked as she stared at the woman she'd thought she knew. They'd gone out for drinks more than a few times, and she and Rebecca had gotten along great. They'd laughed a lot. Rebecca was a couple of years older than Bree, smart as a whip, rich as Croesus, but grounded. Sweet, too. It was one of the mysteries of New York that a woman like her was wanting for dates, but Bree knew that was the truth of it.

"What do you say, Bree? Don't know where he'll take you, but it's bound to be glamorous as all hell."

"I'm from Ohio," Bree said. "I make all my own clothes. Taking the subway is glamorous. He'll get one look at me and fall over laughing."

Rebecca's hand landed on Bree's shoulder. "Don't do that. Come on. That's not you. I wouldn't suggest it if I thought you couldn't hold your own. I've known him my whole life. He's funny. He's smart. You'll like each other. And besides, neither one of you wants more than one night. So what have you got to lose?"

"He's like, the King of Manhattan. What'll I even say?"

"Call him the King of Manhattan. He'll love you forever."

"Don't want forever. But maybe, if people see me with him, even once, they'll remember."

"There'll be pictures," Rebecca said, her focus going back to the pile of cards. "There are always pictures with Charlie."

"What about you?" Bree asked. "See any possibilities in there?"

Rebecca lifted a card. The guy looked yummy, but when she flipped to the back, her expression fell. "One-night stand." She tossed the card back.

"Maybe not," Bree said. "Maybe he only thinks he wants a one-night stand." She kept hold of Charlie's card, knowing if anyone else wanted it, they'd have to pry it out of her cold, dead hand, but picked up the yummy guy's card, as well. "He's a musician. A violinist with the Philharmonic. That's impressive. And he hasn't met you."

Rebecca smiled as she flicked her long tawny hair behind her shoulder. "Are you going to change your mind? Suddenly want marriage and kids from one date with Charlie?"

Bree laughed. "No. Doesn't mean it couldn't happen to someone else."

"Don't worry about me, Kingston. I'll find someone. Let's get you all squared away first. Valentine's night. I'll set it up. Let you know the deets ASAP."

"Oh, God." Bree looked at her outfit. Made on the Singer that shared her closet-cum-bedroom. Hunter-green skirt, lined, with a mod patterned silk blouse, transformed from a thrift store bonanza. Black tights, black heels, a ribbon in her short, short hair. The only thing that had cost any real money were the shoes, and they were secondhand. What if he wanted to go to Pegu Club or 24 Ninth Avenue? Everyone would see instantly that she was a no one from nowhere, wearing nothing that mattered.

"You've got more style in your pinkie than anyone in this room. Than anyone on *Project Runway.* Come on, Bree. This is what you came to New York to do. It's your chance to grab the city by the short hairs. You can do it. I know you can."

Bree straightened her back. "All right. Worst that could happen, I make a complete idiot of myself. I've done that plenty of times. Get Charlie Winslow on the phone. Tell him he's about to meet someone new."

Rebecca laughed. Then she leaned forward just a bit. "You should probably take a breath now, Bree. In fact, maybe we should find a chair. Come on, hon. There's a paper bag right on the counter. That's a girl."

2

Charlie Winslow
Editor in Chief/CEO *Naked New York Media Group*
Studied Business/Marketing at *Harvard University*
Lives in *Manhattan* ❤ Single From *Manhattan*

BREE BLINKED UP AT THE forty-three-story tower at 15 Central Park West, the newest of the luxury, legendary co-op buildings that lined the street across from the park. Just several blocks up were The Dakota, The Majestic and The San Remo. This was quite like being in the center of a very realistic dream. Except that it was freezing. She'd splurged on a taxi even though she'd spent every spare cent on her outfit, using every moment of the trip to talk herself out of a panic attack. The affirmations hadn't been very effective evidently, because even though her date with Charlie Winslow was about to start, she couldn't make her legs move.

She still couldn't believe it. If she hadn't known better, she'd have sworn it was all an elaborate practical joke. Why on earth would Charlie Winslow want to go out with *her?* Of course, she'd asked Rebecca that very question approximately a million times. Bree had gotten a variety of answers, all boiling down to the fact that Rebecca thought the two of them would have a good time.

A good time.

Bree couldn't *move.* Except for her now chattering teeth. The forties era shawl she'd found in Park Slope may have been the perfect accessory, but it did nothing to protect her from the cold. She might as well have worn her gargantuan puffy coat, considering the fact that she was *rooted to the corner of Central Park West and West 72nd Street.*

For God's sake, the most amazing Cinderella night of her life was only moments and a few feet away. She had pictures of this very corner in her New York dream book, the one she'd been compiling for eight years. The only reason Charlie Winslow's photograph hadn't been clipped and pasted was that even her outlandish imagination hadn't been that optimistic.

She had to remember not to call him Charlie Winslow, as if he was a movie star or an historical figure. Bree had practiced. She'd said his first name a hundred times, sometimes laughing, sometimes looking shyly away, coy, sassy, demure, outraged. She was very good at saying *Charlie,* but she couldn't quite help the Winslow part. She'd read so many articles by him and about him, and none of them referred to him as Charlie, or even Mr. Winslow.

She pushed herself forward. If she waited any longer she'd be late, and he'd probably leave without her, which had its merits as then she wouldn't have to endure actually meeting him, but that would defeat the purpose, and dammit, she was brave. She was. She'd gotten on a plane all by herself, knowing absolutely no one in New York, let alone in Manhattan. That took guts.

So did tonight. But she could do it. Because, like her relocation, Charlie Winslow fit perfectly in her five-year plan.

1. Move to New York
2. Get a job in fashion advertising
3. Continue fashion education
4. Find a way into the Inner Circle
5. Become a regular at fashion events
6. ????
7. Publish
8. Success!!!!!!

Look how far she'd come already. She was flying past three directly into four and she'd only been in Manhattan six months! Meeting Charlie Winslow was a piece of cake. The easy part.

Okay, no. That was a total lie. As she headed for the doorman, complete with hat and epaulettes thank you very much, the truth settled like a stone in her stomach. Meeting Charlie Winslow was like meeting the President or Johnny Depp, or Dolce *and* Gabbana.

She would not throw up.

Somehow, the door was opened by the tall man in the cap and gloves, and he smiled at her as he gave her a tiny bow. Then she was inside where it was warm and unbelievably gorgeous. This building wasn't as famous as The Dakota, but it was right up there in the strato-sphere of luxury. Her entire apartment could fit into the reception area where she had to sign in. Everyone smiled. The security guard, the other security guard, the woman by the elevator wearing a winter-white suit, whose huge honkin' diamond ring must make it an effort to lift her hand.

No Charlie Winslow in sight.

Bree let out a breath.

"May I announce your arrival?" The security guard sitting behind the beautiful burnished oak desk leaned forward so elegantly it made her think he was desperate to hear who she was going to see. Either that, or he'd almost lost his grip on the automatic weapon hidden above his lap. Just in case she didn't have the right name or something.

"Bree Kingston for Charlie Winslow," she said, and she only had to clear her throat once.

The way the uniformed man's left eyebrow rose meant something. Bree had no idea what. She glanced down to make sure she hadn't dribbled on her dress, but she appeared fine. If nervous. If very, *very* nervous.

The guard picked up a phone, but his hand stilled midway to his console. He nodded, looking past Bree's shoulder.

She turned, holding her breath, praying she wouldn't make a complete ass of herself. And there he was. Just like his pictures, only better.

Tall, though everyone was tall to her, considering that she barely reached five-one. His hair was as perfectly mussed as it was in his photos—dark, cut with such precision that she imagined he woke up looking camera-ready. He wore a black suit with a simple perfectly tailored white shirt beneath, no tie, slim cut, Yves Saint Laurent? Spencer Hart? Or maybe her beloved D&G?

As gorgeous as the trimmings were, it was his face that snagged and kept her staring. Much, much better than his pictures. Big eyes, brown. Very big. A generous mouth, too, but she kept getting snagged on the eyes, and how he looked as if he'd discovered something wonderful and interesting, except he was looking at her. Smiling big-time. At her.

His gaze let hers go as he took his time across the lobby. Not that it went far: a long slow trip down her body, pausing for a moment on her boobs. Not enough of a pause to make her self-conscious. Any more self-conscious.

She'd been scoped out before, sure. But this felt different. Like an audition. Her heart pounded, blood rushed to heat her cheeks, hell, her whole face. Then he was looking in her eyes again, and she exhaled when he seemed even more pleased. Maybe it was an act, probably was, in fact, but it didn't matter because it was only for one night and she'd imagined dozens of expressions on his face, but none of them had been quite this fantastic.

"Bree," he said, his voice low, a cello kind of baritone full of resonance and promise.

"Hi," she said. "Charlie."

He took her hand in his. The one not holding her clutch, the edge of her shawl. "Rebecca told me you were pretty," he said. "She's never in her life made such an understatement."

Bree's blush went four-alarm and she knew it was a crock, but a gorgeous crock, and if he wanted to say things like that to her for the rest of the night, she wouldn't mind in the least. "You're very kind."

"Not really," he said. Still holding on to her hand, he glanced behind her. "George, could you call for the car?"

"It's in place, Mr. Winslow."

"Thank you," he said, then Charlie looked at her again. "Did she tell you where we're going?"

"She wouldn't. She said I'd like it, though."

"I hope so." He led her out, his hand still holding hers until they got to the exit. When the door was pulled open, Charlie put his arm around her shoulders and picked up the pace. Before she knew it, she was sitting in the backseat of a black limousine driven by an honest-to-God chauffeur and Charlie was scooting in on her left.

How was this her life? Her high school graduating class had under two hundred kids. Seven years later, every one of her friends were married, and most of them had at least one kid. And here she was, being whisked off into a mysterious night with one of the most famous men in New York. On Valentine's Day. Holy mother of pearl.

CHARLIE NORMALLY DIDN'T have champagne chilling in the limo. It had only happened twice before, in fact. Once, when his guest had been a Queen. Not the kind from Asbury Park in New Jersey, but a real royal Queen. The other time had been for a friend who'd been crushed by a devastating loss in the love department. A night of drunken weeping and aimless driving had helped pass the time and given her the courage to face the sunrise.

In tonight's case, he'd ordered the Dom Pérignon Rosé Oenothèque for Rebecca's sake. He knew every detail of the evening would be reported to his cousin, and he was determined to impress Rebecca despite her opinion that he was still the same adolescent terror he'd been at thirteen.

But now that he'd actually met Bree, he wasn't sure

Rebecca deserved such an expensive champagne. Bree was pretty, all right. Petite and sweet-looking with an elfin haircut and a nice little body. But as his date? What was Rebecca thinking?

Clearly there was something more to Bree than his first impression would indicate. Rebecca was bright and she knew him very well. Which meant she knew that the women he went for had mile-long legs, wore nothing but the top labels, were on the cover of *Vogue,* never *Home Sewing Monthly.*

Bree was…tiny. She didn't look terrifically young, just compact. Everything diminutive. There was definitely something appealing in her almond-shaped eyes, heart-shaped face, her pale skin and slight overbite. She was Lula Mae before she became Holly Golightly, and where they were headed? She would be a guppy out of water.

He was almost afraid to speak to her, not having the first clue what to say. He was just a vain enough idiot to have loved the way her eyes had widened at meeting him, how she'd trembled, although that could have been from the cold. But that rush could only last so long. Some champagne would help both of them.

She turned from the window as he popped the cork. "I didn't know that was a real thing," she said. "Champagne in a limousine."

"It's decadent and foolish, but then this is Valentine's Day. Besides, we're not driving, so what the hell."

"No, we're not. I should warn you, I'm not much of a drinker."

"We'll have to be judicious with our ordering, then. But how about one drink, to christen the adventure ahead?"

She stared at the crystal flute in his hand. "Yes, thank you. I'd like that."

"There will always be tonic, soda or juice wherever we are, although you'll be surrounded by booze." He filled her glass, careful what with the stop-and-go traffic. "If you tell me what you prefer, I'll make sure you have it."

"I like pineapple juice the best," she said, taking the glass from him with her slender hand, her nails trim and shiny and pale.

"Pineapple it is." He poured himself a glass then sat back, lifting the flute to hers. "To blind dates."

Her smile did nice things to her face. Made it clear she hadn't learned to hold back yet, to equate cynicism with sophistication. He hadn't seen that in a long while. Not up close.

"To extraordinary things," she replied, clicking his glass gently.

The champagne was excellent, perfectly cold and just dry enough. "Tell me about yourself, Bree," he said, leaning back into his corner of the seat. He didn't want to crowd her or make her uncomfortable. They had a big night ahead of them, and as long as she was his date, he truly wanted to show her a good time. Nothing extravagant, naturally. Experience had taught him it was better to stay low-key with new people of any stripe. Since the success of *Naked New York,* he'd had to relearn public navigation.

His celebrity could still be an awkward fit, although nothing like it had been when the business had hit critical mass. He'd set out to make a name, but when he'd first put the blog plan together, he envisioned himself more like a Jason Weisberger of BoingBoing than an Arianna Huffington. Someone whose name would be recognized by people who mattered, but who was not easily recognized in person. Instead, he'd become part of a new phenomena. In Manhattan, more people recognized him than recognized the mayor. Financially, it was the best thing that could have happened. Personally, it had been…interesting and not terrifically pleasant.

Bree turned her lovely green eyes to her glass, watching the bubbles pop and fizz. "I'm a copywriter," she said. "At BBDA. A baby copywriter, which means I'm mostly a gofer and I take a lot of notes, type a lot of memos. But it's good. The people I work with are quick and creative and they aren't out for blood. Well, not more than you'd expect."

"BBDA is a big firm. A number of their clients advertise on my blogs."

Her eyes widened again. "Seventeen of them, at the moment. *Naked New York* is a major focus in the eighteen-to-thirty-four demographic."

The last word had been bitten off, and she pressed her lips together for a second. "Anyway," she said, her voice lower, slower. "I graduated last year with an MBA from Case Western. I'd always wanted to come to New York, so I did."

"Is New York what you thought it would be?"

"Much better. I loved it even before tonight."

He laughed.

"Come on, you have to know how much this evening is blowing the bell curve. You're Charlie Winslow and we're going on a mystery date, and even though I have no idea where, I'm sure it's going to be the most thrilling night of my life."

He couldn't help his wince, although he tried not to. "Most thrilling? That's a tall order."

She lowered her head, frowned a bit, then looked up at him through her long lashes. "Really? This—" she waved at the lush interior of the car, at, he imagined, the night in general "—is insane. It may be your day-to-day, but it's certainly not mine." Bree sat back, sipped the cold champagne. "Rebecca wouldn't tell me. Every time I asked why you'd want to go out with me on Valentine's night, for God's sake, she smiled in that smug way that made me want to pinch her."

He smiled. "You know, I find myself wanting to pinch Rebecca a lot."

"Then you'll understand my frustration when I ask you straight-out, why are we doing this? Why are *you* doing this with *me?* I can't help thinking it might be some awful mean-girl prank. That wherever we're going, there'll be a big spotlight on me when I'm covered in green slime or something. Which would be horrible by the way. In case you need to call ahead."

Okay. She made him laugh. Big point in the plus column. And now that she'd admitted her fear, she seemed more relaxed. Now that he'd noticed, he lingered on the way her simple sleeveless dress showed off the woman more than the garment. He liked that she wore no jewelry. It was a bold choice, but it brought his focus to her neck, which had more appeal than a neck had any right to. There was just something about her skin, the way her chin curved, her elegant clavicle. There was a thought he'd never expected to have.

"Rebecca isn't like that," Bree said, softer now, more to herself than him, and Charlie remembered she'd asked him why he'd pursued the date.

Before he could answer, she added, "I haven't known her for long, so maybe I'm wrong, but my instincts are pretty good, and she stood out right from the start."

Bree used her hand again, not a wave this time, but a flip of the wrist. A tiny wrist, delicate and feminine.

"We went for drinks this one night at Caracas, Rebecca and me and our friend Lilly, who teaches music at this amazingly exclusive prep school, and it started out a little weird, because the three of us only knew each other from the lunch exchange, but then we started talking and we clicked, especially Rebecca and me. When I mentioned how desperately I'd wanted to live in Manhattan, both of them completely got it. How I don't mind paying a fortune to live in the Black Hole of Calcutta with four girls I barely know, and how I can't even afford to go to a movie, let alone have popcorn. They grinned and we toasted each other with sidecars, and I felt as if I was home." Bree blinked and then for some reason her shoulders stiffened again. She cleared her throat. "That may have gotten away from me a little."

And…he liked her. Just like that. No, she wasn't his type, not even close, but he liked the cadence of her speech, the way she talked with her hands, how she was clearly nervous but not cowed. The night changed right then, between Columbus Avenue and West 61st.

Charlie touched her arm. She was warm and soft, and she flinched a bit at the contact, catching herself with a breath and a smile.

"No," he said, "it's not a prank or a trick. Rebecca thought we'd get along. She and I grew up together, were friends through private schools and first dates and proms and way too many horrific holiday celebrations." He shuddered thinking about some of the epic Christmases, the ones where half the family wasn't speaking to the other half, where feuds were conducted across air-kisses and designer wreaths. All that passive-aggressive power brokering over Beluga caviar and shaved truffles. "She knows me as well as anyone. And she's never wanted to set me up before."

"So what does that mean?"

He thought for a second. Excellent question. "I don't know."

Instead of pressing him for his best guess, Bree's head tilted fetchingly. "Where are we going?"

"You don't want to be surprised?"

The way she looked at him made him want to meet her expectations, even though there was no way he could. "I've been stunned since you took my hand."

Stunned? "What were you expecting?"

She shrugged. "Not sure. Something else. I mean, I'm not shocked about the doormen, the limousine or how amazing you smell, because I was secretly hoping for all that. I've never been around celebrities much. I've seen some since I've been here. The obligatory Woody Allen sighting, of course, but there've been others. Quite a few of them, now that I think about it, but they've all seemed, I don't know, extraordinary. In the truest sense of the word. As if the air around them was sparkly, or that even if they looked like they'd thrown on a potato sack and bowling shoes, it was on purpose, but I wasn't cool enough to get it. You're not like that."

"Is that a compliment?"

She nodded. "Yes. It would have been okay if you'd turned out to be a major hipster, although I definitely would have bored you to tears."

Charlie grinned. "Know how many hipsters it takes to screw in a lightbulb?"

She grinned back, leaning in for the punch line. "How many?"

He purposely rolled his eyes. "Some really obscure number you've never even heard of."

Bree laughed. It started out as delicate as her wrist, but ended in an unexpected snort. Her eyes widened and she held her hand up in front of her face, but then she did it again. The snort, not the laugh. And she added a blush that was the most honest thing he'd seen in years.

Okay, Rebecca might deserve more than a sparkling wine. The vote was still out if she'd end up with a '96 Krug Clos D'Ambonnay.

3

BREE KNEW SHE WAS BLUSHING, but there wasn't a single solitary thing she could do about it. From the way Charlie was smiling at her, the problem wasn't going to fix itself anytime soon.

She wished they'd get to wherever they were going. She needed some distance, just for a moment. A bathroom stall would work, a private place where she could squeal and jump and act like a fool and get it out of her system. Because *whoa*. Charlie Winslow plus limo plus champagne plus the fact that his dates always ended with more than a friendly peck on the cheek and she was practically levitating. The whole night, no matter where they ended up, was improbably perfect. Her once in a lifetime.

Someone had reached into her fantasies, reviewed those that were most outlandish and most frequent, decided they weren't grand enough then given her *this*. She wanted to lean over the front seat and ask the driver, a nice-looking guy she'd guess was in his fifties, if he had a video camera, and would he mind filming every second of the rest of the night so she could watch it until her eyes fell out.

She glanced out the window and all her thoughts stuttered to a halt. "This is Lincoln Center," she said, her voice high and tight.

"It is," Charlie said, and while she couldn't take her eyes off the scene in front of her, she could hear the amusement in his voice.

"It's Lincoln Center," she repeated, "and this is *Fashion Week*."

"Right again."

"It was in the blog. This morning. I read it. This is the Mercedes-Benz/Vogue party for Fashion Week."

She wanted to open the window, stick her head out like an overexcited puppy so she could see *everything*. But she might as well paint a sign on her forehead that said *hick*. Still, she couldn't help it if her hands shook, if her breath fogged the window, if she wanted to pinch herself to prove she was really, really here.

"I thought you might have guessed." His voice sounded smiley. Not smirky, though, and she would have thought...

"No." She grinned. "No, really. No. It's too much. Come on. It's...fashion Nirvana. The single event after which I could die happy." She turned, briefly, to gape at him, to verify the smile she'd guessed at. "I've been sewing since I was twelve."

Then she was staring again, at the klieg lights, at the people. Glittering, gorgeous, famous, glamorous people. Her heroes and heroines. In one small clump standing near a police barricade there were three, *THREE,* designers. Designers she adored, well, maybe not *her,* because she was kind of derivative, but still, Bree was going to be in the same room, at the same party as Tommy Hilfiger, as Vivienne Westwood!

She turned again to Charlie, almost spilling her drink. "We are going to the party, right?"

"Yeah, we're going to the party."

"Oh, thank God. That would have been really embarrassing. If we were going to a concert or something."

He laughed in a way that made her shiver and reminded her again that this wasn't a dream. The limo was in a long line of limos, and Bree guessed it would be a while until it was their turn. Which meant that she had a window of alone-time with Charlie. She leaned back in the luxurious leather seat so he was the center of her attention. "I remember reading about this last year. It sounded as if you had a good time."

He nodded. "I did, considering it's part of the job. I think this year will be better." He spoke casually, as if they were talking about stopping at the corner market. As if they knew each other. Casually, but not bored or above it all. This was a typical night for him. A night to look forward to but not to panic over.

Speaking of panic. "We're at Fashion Week, and I'm wearing a homemade dress. My shawl…" It had cost fifty cents at the thrift shop but he didn't have to know *that*. "Oh, God."

He studied her, grinning. She couldn't tell if it was because he thought she looked adorably out of her league or laughably ridiculous. When he leaned forward, Bree wasn't sure what to do until he crooked his finger for her to move in closer. Conspiratorially closer. "The whole point of fashion is originality and talent. Everyone will look at you, at your dress, and wonder who the new designer is. I suggest you milk that till the cow's dry."

She had to laugh, because well… "That's a very nice thing to say." She touched the back of his hand to make sure he knew she wasn't kidding, only the second her hand was on his, she realized how they were mere inches apart. She could feel his breath on her cheek, the warmth of his body sneaking into her own.

That he could think she was capable of pulling off something so outrageous was…awesome. "I'm not sure I could keep a straight face."

"Look bored," he said. "That's the key. Act as if you'd rather be anywhere else on earth, and they'll all think you're the next big thing."

"Bored. I can do bored." She had to lean back a bit because being this close to Charlie was making it hard not to hyperventilate. "Actually, no, I can't, not here. My God, no one's that good an actress. But I can be observant. Which almost looks like bored."

He moved back, too, his smile lingering in the way his eyes crinkled. "Observant can work. Remember, though, that there's no one here you need to be intimidated by. Well, almost. But you probably won't meet them, anyway."

Oh, he was good. This was effortless charm, the true heart of tact and perfect manners. To put her at ease as they inched their way to the Mount Everest of her aspirations? Wonderful, wonderful. But she'd better bring herself down a notch, because at this height, a fall could kill her. "I read an article once," she said, "by a woman whose passion was movies, and she went and got herself a job in the business. She said that in the end it was kind of sad. That what she'd loved were the illusions, the characters, the fantasy. Once she'd looked behind the curtain it was never the same again."

Charlie finished off his champagne and put his flute back in the space next to the ice bucket, slowly, as if he were giving deliberate thought to what she'd said. "I can see that. Most terribly brilliant people I've known are also terribly troubled. Not all of them, but a lot of them."

"I don't think I'll be disappointed. I know it's all illusion. And that's okay with me. I had normal. A whole hell of a lot of normal. It wasn't for me."

"Where was that?" he asked. "Your normal."

"Ohio," she said. "Little tiny town. Great big family. Happy. Well-adjusted. My folks had lots of siblings, I have lots of siblings, everyone else in my family wants to get married, if they aren't already, have a bunch of kids, live within driving distance of the family home. We're a Norman Rockwell relic, with small rebellions and modest dreams. I can't tell you how much I hated it. Not my family, they're great, but that life. Knowing what the day would bring. The Sunday dinners and the baby showers, knowing every person at the Cline's SuperValu and never having to look at the menu at Yoders. I wanted out."

She took in a deep breath of Manhattan limousine air. "I want unpredictability and crowds of people, all of them in a rush. I want to go to clubs and stay out till 4:00 a.m. when I have to be at work at eight and I want to eat things I can't pronounce and I want to have my heart broken by callous men who wear gorgeous suits."

She looked away, feeling foolish. Talk about TMI. It was all nerves, of course, but there was no way not to be nervous given the circumstances. The line of limos, hiding their secret passengers, was still impressive.

"I think you'll be great here," Charlie said, and it occurred to her that the timbre of his voice wasn't the biggest surprise, the kindness was. "They're all divas, and what do divas do best?"

"Get free swag?"

Charlie laughed as he shook his head. "They think about themselves. They'll be far too preoccupied to focus much attention on you. The only reason they'll notice me is because they can use me. So relax. Enjoy it. You'll have a great time."

She was already having the time of her life, and they hadn't left the car, so the possibility of enjoying herself for the rest of the night wasn't out of the question. She wouldn't necessarily trip or spill something down her dress. She'd already decided she would eat nothing that could possibly get stuck in her teeth. And she'd make sure she didn't get drunk.

Charlie leaned forward until he had his driver's attention. "We're going to be at least a few hours, Raymond," he said. "Feel free to leave. I'll give you some warning when it looks like we're ready to go."

"Will do, Mr. Winslow. Thanks."

Bree shook her head. When she'd first come to the city she'd been prepared for mass rudeness, cynicism and impatience from every corner. Hadn't happened. Not that there weren't more than a fair share of asshats in residence, but the proportions had been off. Mostly the people she'd met, whether it was asking for directions or standing on line at Starbucks, had been nice. Pleasant. They could be brusque but they were more than willing to help, even when she hadn't asked. Those were the regular folks, though, not people like Charlie. If television shows about rich New Yorkers were to be believed, he should have been a complete bastard.

Instead, he'd brought her to *Fashion Week*. She'd been a slave to fashion since seventh grade. Her walls had been covered with her collages, a perfect pair of shoes from *Vogue,* with a particular skirt from *W* and a top from *Seventeen.* Of course, there'd been photos of accessories included, affixed with Mod Podge and shellacked so they'd be permanent reminders that she had more than a daydream. She had a goal.

Her love of writing had come later, and the combination? That had been a match made in heaven. Her destiny was set—she'd be a style writer, a trendsetter, a goddess of form and function.

To be here with Charlie was…nope. No words came close to what this felt like.

The man himself shifted in the seat so he could watch her, but also have a clear view through her window. "It's a hell of a culture shock, moving to New York," he said. "A lot of people find nothing but trouble in Manhattan."

"I wouldn't mind finding a little trouble," she said, a blush stealing up her cheeks. She touched her purse, hyperaware of the thong, the toothbrush, the condom and the rest that made up her one-night stand kit. Rebecca hadn't said it outright, but she hadn't needed to. Charlie's bachelor ways were the stuff of legend.

The theme from *Mission Impossible* rang from her purse, scaring the crap out of her.

"I bet I know who that is," he said.

Bree opened her clutch, not wanting him to see her kit, or, heaven forbid, his trading card. She snatched her phone and saw she had a message from Rebecca.

U there yet?

Bree grinned.

!!!!!!!

Knew U 2 wld be gr8

We'll talk tomrw I ❤ u for this!

You're welcome. Knock m dead!

Charlie tried to sneak a peek, and she helped him by turning her screen.

He pulled his own phone out of his jacket pocket. Of course it was something amazing looking. Might have been a BlackBerry, she thought, latest gen at the very least, if not some exotic model not available to the public. Unlike her second-hand first-gen iPhone.

He was amazingly fast with his thumbs. Dexterous. But his texting couldn't hold a candle to how expressive his face was. He grinned in a whole different way than he had a moment ago. None of that sweet, reflective rumination. Now he was the very picture of high amusement, his head tilted to the side, his eyebrows raised in either surprise or delight, possibly both. Or maybe something completely different, but this was the night for believing the best, right?

Before she put her phone back, she turned it so she had his face framed for a quick photo. She'd be damned if she wasn't going home with some physical mementoes from tonight, and no, blisters from her incredibly high heels didn't count.

As she reached to put her cell in her bag, it hit her. Why she was here. Why Rebecca had given her Charlie's card. What the whole deal was.

A favor.

First night out with Rebecca, Bree had spilled her five-year plan all over the conversation. Her dreams, the steps, the obsession. Rebecca hadn't told her she was related to Charlie. Hadn't seemed to be aware of Fashion Week at all. That sneaky…

Which meant Bree had better pull her expectations down another fifty notches. She wasn't really on a *date* with Charlie. She was on a favor. Those two things ended in completely different ways. Favors didn't extend to the bedroom.

Charlie put his phone back in his jacket pocket just as her phone beeped again. "It's going to be crowded in there. I've just sent you my number. If we get separated, text me, and I'll find you."

She had Charlie Winslow's cell phone number. She could be excited about that. It might be a one-off, but so what? Just because it was a favor didn't mean it wasn't the biggest kick of her life.

"You okay?" he asked.

"Fine. Great. Am I likely to lose you?"

"Not if I can help it—ah, we're here."

The door next to Bree opened as Charlie slipped her glass from between her fingers. In yet another spectacular fairy-tale moment, she stepped onto a red carpet. She hadn't flashed anyone, she hadn't tripped and she managed not to let her jaw drop even when flashbulbs popped all around, blinding and thrilling in equal measure.

Charlie took hold of her arm above her elbow, and that was good because she really couldn't see a thing. People around her were shouting, "Over here!" and "Look up!" over and over, and she hadn't anticipated so much noise. Whenever she watched this part on TV it was silent, a voice-over, then a cut to a commercial, but here it was loud and scary and intrusive.

Charlie's hand squeezed gently as he escorted her toward a towering white tent, which she knew was the

Fashion Week venue in Damrosch Park. The area was huge, with runway shows from morning till night, cocktail parties, dining areas, meeting rooms, press rooms.

She'd been here, to Lincoln Center, but on the other side, with the fountain and the Met and the magic staircase. To be here now, when the whole complex was dressed up in its fancy best, when to get inside the tents should have been impossible for a girl like her, was a lot to process.

Thank goodness for Charlie's steadying hand. What world was she in that the most comforting thing around her was Charlie Winslow? She honestly couldn't tell if she was trembling more from the freezing cold or the excitement.

There was so much to look at between flashes of light, she was shocked to step inside. There was a line, and because this was the real world, there were metal detectors to go through. No one seemed to mind, though. Security was tight, and the slower pace as they were herded forward gave her a chance to catch her breath, only to lose it again as she got a load of who she was standing near.

Charlie's breath warmed her neck as he leaned in close. Goose bumps. Everywhere. Down her spine and up her arms. When his voice followed, low and warm, her own breath hitched and her eyes may have rolled up in her head for just a second. Probably in a minute she'd get with the program. She wouldn't feel faint from his touch, or by standing one person away from her favorite designer on earth. The problem was, she couldn't decide what to stare at—the clothes or the designers themselves. Oh, God, there was the model who was on the cover of this month's issue of *Elle,* and good God almighty, that was the star of her favorite CSI, and Bree was so grateful for Charlie's arm.

"You'll never see more food go to waste than you will at this party," Charlie said in that same intimate whisper he'd used in the limo. "I don't think any of these people actually eat. They do chew a lot of gum, though. Ketosis. It's a breath thing, not that you'll ever hear about it in *Vogue* or *W.* People who don't eat may look fantastic on camera, but their breath could kill a buffalo. Be warned."

Bree giggled, and while it was true that everyone in the two long lines snaking into the tent was on the ridiculous side of thin, most of the people she saw were subtly chewing, or standing in such a way as to avoid being breathed upon.

Of course, she thought of her own breath now. She'd barely eaten today, too nervous.

"You're fine," he said, with a minty-scented chuckle. "Don't fret."

She smiled at him as they inched along. "I guess I'm not hiding my small-town roots very well, huh?"

"I don't know what you mean."

She gave him a knowing look. "I'll try harder to appear blasé."

"Don't do that for my sake." Charlie tugged her around even more, until they were facing each other. "I like that this is magical for you."

"I'm a real novelty, huh?"

"Truthfully, yes. But a good one. I want to hear much, much more about your life before New York. I'm a native, and the way I was raised, you'd think there wasn't anything between California and New York. I've never been to Ohio, although I'm reasonably sure

I could point to it on a map. It's at the bottom of Lake Erie, right?"

"Wow, I'm impressed. Yeah."

"And where in Ohio did you grow up?"

She waved her hand at him and turned to check on the line's progress. "You've never heard of it." When she looked back, his smile was a bit crooked. "So that food you mentioned. Passed around on little trays? Buffet? Sit down banquet?"

"The first two," he said. "There will be places to sit, tables all around, and here's a secret. You can completely tell the pecking order by who sits, who stands and where those two things happen."

Her eyes widened at yet another morsel of insider-y goodness. She felt as if he was giving her the ultimate backstage pass, and while she knew a lot of it had to do with manners and even more to do with Rebecca, there was a tiny flare of hope buried deep inside that perhaps he was letting her in because he liked her? A little?

Probably a good idea not to linger on that thought. She needed to be in the moment, enjoying the hell out of what she had. To ask for anything more was tempting fate.

4

CHARLIE COULDN'T TAKE his eyes off Bree. What had Rebecca seen that had made her believe this absurd blind date could work? That it was working was…bizarre. He never would have guessed he would find Bree enchanting.

Hell, that he found anything enchanting stretched credulity.

And yet, watching her reminded him what it was like when he'd had heroes. Though he'd never been as innocently enthralled by glamour as Bree. Given his background, how could he have been? His family was part of xenophobic wealthy New York, the inbred, insane inner circle that made disdain and dismissal an art form. So his heroes had been those outside the fold: sports stars, indie musicians who would never be mainstream, oddball scientists and computer hackers. The last, thank goodness, had actually set in motion key aspects of his life.

"Oh, God," Bree whispered, her hand clasping desperately at his lapel. "That's Mick Jagger."

Charlie followed her gaze a few feet away to where the old warhorse stood, surrounded by his all-but-invisible-to-him entourage. The Rolling Stone hadn't been there a few minutes ago, but there wasn't a person in the tent, hell in the city, that would call him out for cutting in line.

"Huh," Bree said, still staring curiously at the mega-star.

"Better get used to that," Charlie said, enjoying himself. The past couple of years, the novelty of his lifestyle had dulled. He rarely considered anything outside of the job. Who to interview, who to keep an eye on, who was ready for a career obit. Filling Bree in was fun. She'd been right. No way she could pass for bored. Not even close. "Almost everyone's shorter than you think," he continued, stepping closer to her. "The men, especially. Not the models, though, they're giraffes, but the actors, the musicians? Most of them are even shorter than I am."

"You're not," Bree said. She turned and laid a smile on him that made him feel like a giant. "*I'm* short. Ridiculously so. It's awful."

"Why awful?"

Her smile changed and the tips of her ears turned pink. "I'm twenty-five, not twelve. Everyone thinks I'm cute. And harmless. Like a baby bunny. I've had people pat me on the head. I mean, come on. Who does that?"

"Not me," he said, holding his hands up and away, mostly because now that she'd said it, he wanted to.

"I want to take his picture," she said, lowering her voice as she stole glances at Jagger.

"So? Take it."

She shook her head. "And that would advance my agenda of being a bored new designer how? I'm already an outsider. I'd like to at least pretend for a bit."

Charlie turned to the person in back of him, some

guy he didn't know, but who looked like he might be a reporter. "We'll be back in a sec, okay?"

The guy nodded, and Charlie kept his grip on Bree's arm as he crossed over to the other line, right smack in the middle of the rock stars' party. "Hey, Mick," he said, holding out his hand. "Charlie Winslow. I'd love to get a photograph with you and my lovely date. Do you mind?"

The man shook Charlie's hand, but only smiled once he set eyes on Bree. Then he couldn't have been nicer. In fact, before they'd been there two minutes, Jagger had his arm around Bree's shoulders and Charlie was taking the photo with her phone.

Bree looked thrilled to her toes even when Jagger copped a surreptitious feel during the photo op. Charlie wasted no time escorting her back to their saved place.

"I have to see," she whispered, pressing buttons on her cell. "My hands are shaking. I'm such a dork."

He took over the delicate operation, and she oohed and aahed at her fantastic luck. She was trembling with excitement and he would never have guessed. When she'd stood with one of the biggest celebrities on the planet, she'd appeared completely cool about the whole affair. Now her eyes hid nothing of her excitement. She grinned widely and clapped her hands together like a kid at the circus. Which, he supposed, she was.

Then they were at the security checkpoint, and there were wands and buckets and well-behaved guards. A short walk across a cold path, and they entered the main tent, the vast pavilion filled with music and chatter and laughter and a hundred different perfumes. Dresses that cost more than cars, faces that had been sculpted to the point of madness, lots of skin, lots of white teeth, and Bree looking like she'd arrived in Wonderland.

Charlie tried not to stare at her as they weaved through the crowd, as some chart topper sang her country tunes and photographs were taken. He sent a waiter for pineapple juice, and when he handed it to Bree, she blinked in utter bemusement.

It was too entertaining to last, because while he was on a date, he was also on assignment, and at least fifty percent of the guests at this shindig wanted their names on his blog tomorrow.

Normally this dance was one he could do in his sleep. Tonight, though, he wanted not just to include Bree, but feature her, make sure she met everyone she recognized. He wanted to see what she'd do, how she'd react. Unexpected. Completely out of character for him and puzzling, but nothing he cared to examine.

He felt drawn to Bree, which hadn't happened in so long he'd almost forgotten it could happen. What was more interesting was that he couldn't pinpoint why. If he had his way, he'd spend more time figuring out the deal with Bree than getting the dirt on the A-listers at the party.

"What's wrong?" After a tour of the immediate area, complete with air kisses, handshakes, posturing and pumped-up drama, they found a spot as far away from the speakers as they could get. Yet even next to the side exits to the powder rooms and private paths, Bree had to shout.

"Nothing. You having a good time?"

"Yes," she said. "Although I'm still in shock. It's overwhelming."

"It is. There are a lot of people wanting attention."

"I see what you mean about the seats," she said as she scooted closer to him.

He slipped his arm around her waist. Interesting, holding someone who was so small. He felt… protective.

"It's as if every chair is a throne, exclusively for the most important kings and queens."

He nodded. "Some of them have a seat for a lifetime, but not many. For most of them, it's a limited run."

"You could sit," she said. "You probably do, don't you?"

"Nope. I work the room. I may be recognizable to some, but my job here is to shine a light on the real celebrities. I'll have to blog this in the morning, and if I don't get it right, I'll get dozens of calls and texts and emails from furious PR people telling me I'm a disgrace and I'll never work in this town again."

A waiter carrying champagne came by, and before Charlie could say anything, Bree touched his hand. "I'd like one, please."

"Sure?"

She nodded. "It's a champagne night."

"You must be starving. I haven't seen you eat a thing."

"I'm too excited to eat. I shook hands with Tim Gunn!"

"I know," he said. "He liked what you were wearing."

"He did not," Bree said, almost spilling her drink. "Why, did he say something?" She closed her eyes. "No, don't answer that. You're being sweet."

"Yeah, but if he'd had a minute to notice, he would have liked your dress. You look stunning."

She sighed. "I didn't expect you," she said. "To be honest, I'm not even sure what to make of you."

"What does that mean?"

"I know I'm not at all what you're used to. Yesterday, I saw a picture of you with Mia Cavendish. Then I saw her on the new Victoria's Secret billboard in Times Square. Rebecca went way above and beyond doing me this favor, but you've made tonight incredible. A dream come true. I don't even…"

He hadn't thought of it in the car, or in line, or after the Jagger incident, but right now, he couldn't think of anything in the world he wanted more than to pull this tiny person into his arms and kiss the daylights out of her.

So he did.

BREE SHOULDN'T HAVE BEEN shocked by his lips, but she froze, stunned more completely than she'd been at being bumped by Jean Paul Gaultier. *Charlie Winslow* was kissing *her*. Softly. Teasing her with the tip of his tongue, waiting for permission to enter.

She obliged.

He turned out to be a gentleman in this respect, as well. No thrusting, no swallowing her whole. Entering slowly, he gave her time to get used to him. To savor. She'd expected champagne but he tasted like mint, although come to think of it, she had no idea what the finish of champagne would taste like.

One flat palm touched her bare shoulder, his other hand pulled her closer, and the tentative portion of the kiss ended, as did all but the most basic of thoughts. He angled his head and settled in for a stay as they explored each other. It didn't take long for her shoulders to relax, to feel comfortable enough to pull back for a breath and a peek, then return for more.

That hand on her shoulder moved across her back warming her wherever it touched. It wasn't cold in the room, not with this many people, but Charlie's touch felt hot, not only his hand, either. The bass from the band made the room vibrate but she was already quivering. Kissing Prince Charming did that to a person.

As if the night wasn't spectacular enough.

She'd never forget this, the song that was playing, how she felt him moan even though she couldn't hear him. It was dizzying, every part of it, and her hope that this was more than just a favor went from not daring to think it to letting the idea take a seat.

He pulled back, not very far. "As much as I'd like to stay right here, I have to work. I'll warn you now, the people we're going to meet won't pay you enough attention. They're working the room, as well."

"I don't mind," she said truthfully. She expected nothing from this crowd. Which couldn't be said about Charlie. She had to stop herself from touching her mouth like a lovesick tween, but God, he had great lips. No matter how she looked at it, there'd been no reason to kiss her, none at all, except he'd wanted to. There went her breath, and any hope of walking on her wobbly knees.

"A room this size, it's going to take a couple of hours. Make sure at some point that you get something to eat. I won't be able to look after you as carefully as I'd like, and we can't have you keeling over from starvation. Grab things when you can, or duck out to the buffet. I'll be holding my cell, so I'll hear if you call, and we'll find each other."

She nodded. "Go. Work. Do your magic. I was always excited to read your Fashion Week blogs. You made me feel as if I was there."

"Really?"

"Well, now that I'm here, not exactly, but more than

enough. Don't tell, but I like your reports better than the ones in *W*."

He grinned. "Now you're just being nice."

"Nope." She crossed her heart. "Mean every word."

"Come on, then. Let's go meet some famous people."

Bree was tempted to pull him in for one more kiss, to make sure it had been real, but didn't dare. Although it was hard not to imagine what it would feel like to walk across the lobby of his building, to go up in that elevator. Before her foolish notions got too carried away, she was reminded, quite spectacularly, of what she was doing now. A boatload of iconic symbols had come to life.

She felt like a Lilliputian in a world of Gullivers with Charlie as her guide. He led her through paths between tables, ice sculptures dripping and corks popping, and always, always the intrusion of cameras. Around the perimeter of the party, the different celebrity gossip shows had staked their territories, and their camera lighting bounced off the white of the tent making the entire arena glow.

They would walk two, maybe three steps, then stop as another celebrity, each one a surprise, approached Charlie. Interestingly, none of the familiar faces looked quite right. They were either better or shorter or skinnier or blonder than they looked in *People* or on TV.

Bree was good with makeup. Really. She'd made a point of learning the correct techniques at a beauty school near her college, but there was an element of magic to the faces that passed by. And the clothes…

She'd browsed through some of the high-end boutiques in Manhattan. D&G, of course, but a few couture houses, as well, showcasing their elegantly crafted suits and dresses, not daring to touch because each button or zip was worth more than everything she owned or would own for years to come. Now she saw those creations in motion, and it was poetry. No way to call it anything other than art. Each designer's style was as individual as a Picasso or a Rembrandt. She felt humbled. And grabby.

Instead of touching the fifty-thousand dollar gown, she snagged some hors d'oeuvres. Prawns and sushi and filet mignon, each with a little napkin and dabs of aioli. If she hadn't been an adult person standing next to famous people she wouldn't have stopped shoving them into her mouth because they were *fantastic.* The champagne was chilled, and she should switch back to pineapple juice because even with the food her edges were sliding toward fuzzy.

She turned to Charlie, only Charlie wasn't there. Not where she'd left him, but that had been before she'd followed the hamachi tray, dammit. She did a complete three-sixty, pausing as she saw clumps of celebrities, and that made her giggle, because certainly clumps wasn't the proper collective. What was? A cavalcade of celebs? A coterie? An ensemble? No, a *superficiality* of celebrities. Ha.

Bree pulled out her cell phone, pulled up Charlie's cell number and typed. *You're not here.*

He could be anywhere, so it wouldn't hurt to meander. Maybe get a small bottle of water. Her cell would vibrate when he texted back, so she could work on her Not From Hicksville Face as she gasped to herself.

Where are you? CW

Standing next to 1 of the Olsen twins. Not sure which 1. Doesn't matter.

Not able to find you via Olsen twin. Something more stationary please? CW

Ah. Stella McCartney holding court.

Perfect. But can't leave quite yet. Ten min. CW

Who are you with? Nvr mind. Ur busy.

Bree lowered her phone, but it dinged.

3 people who want in. 2 who'll get in. 0 fun as U. CW

She flushed with pleasure, even though it was a line, nothing more, and yet she'd never delete that text ever.

❤

The second she pressed Send, Bree panicked. It was a heart. She meant he was being sweet. Not— Oh, crap, he'd probably—

Um. I meant thank U.

☺ CW

She exhaled, still freaked out enough to barely glance at the second Olsen twin. She switched contacts, and texted.

Rebecca, I screwed up.

How?

Sent him ❤

???

SENT HIM ❤!!!!!

No worries. He won't mind.

But—

Hush. Trust me. & smile

The ding from a different text happened. Charlie.

Stay by Stella ETA 2 min CW

Bree decided to believe Rebecca and smile. Then she dialed the grin down from eleven to a reasonable five. Her heart, however, wasn't so cooperative. It was a silly mistake, that's all. Not even a mistake. A ❤ didn't have to mean anything significant. She used it with her friends all the time, and they didn't think she was declaring her undying love.

She was nervous, that's all. The atmosphere, the date itself. The *Olsens*.

And what came next. What *might* come next.

As a sneak peek, the kiss held great promise. She liked Charlie more than she'd expected to, and he'd kissed her, so he didn't find her repulsive or anything, so that was a point in her favor. Truthfully? She was equal parts good-anxious and insanely terrified-anxious about spending time alone with him. But first time—only time—sex with anyone was scary. So much potential for catastrophe. The ♥ was nothing compared to all the things that could go wrong.

She'd had her fair share of errors in the bedroom. The memories of which made her blush. But now was not the time to brood about mistakes made when learning the ins and outs, so to speak, of sex with relative strangers. It was the time to look for Charlie, to appreciate every single moment of being here, in this miraculous room, with a date that made her nipples take note, favor or not.

There were no twins at all around her now, but Ms. McCartney had a very large and enthusiastic crowd around her, and it was easy to see why. Although she couldn't hear the designer, or even see her face very well, the people within ear and eyeshot were smiling. Not the kind of smile that made a person shiver, the kind that erased years and made it fun to eavesdrop. But there was Charlie, and his smile....

God.

That was something. If it was fake, she'd take it, hands down over many other genuine things in life. Somehow, though, she didn't think it was fake. No matter, she grinned back, honest as the day was long. It wasn't that he was the most handsome man she'd ever seen. There were a number here tonight who would look better on a magazine cover. Of course, they were models, so that made sense. Charlie's charm was in the reality of his face. There were lines, small ones, that would have been airbrushed out on a cover, but she liked them. They gave him character and made him look as suave as he was. They were smile lines, which were always a good sign. Especially on the King of Manhattan.

She liked that he was thirty-one. Men in their twenties could have…issues. Fine, no problem, she was in her twenties and could make lists of all the things she wished were different, so no throwing stones, but guys were boys longer than women were girls, that was a fact. Charlie would be a wonderful lover, she imagined as she met him halfway to the dessert spread. That kiss had been an amuse-bouche. The meal would be like heaven.

"You look relatively unscathed," Charlie said. "I'm shocked."

"Why?"

"I'd have thought every straight man in the building would have been all over you."

"Stop."

"Not a line," he said. "I mean it. I'm stunned. I rushed. Although I figured you could take care of yourself."

"Based on?"

"Everything I've seen so far. You and Mick Jagger, for instance." Charlie slipped his hand across her lower back. "What would you like to see next?"

Bree met his gaze. "The view from here is fine."

He sighed, and because there was a momentary pause in the music, she heard it. The live music had stopped a while ago, and now there was recorded stuff—the mix excellent. Of course they'd have a great DJ at a party like this.

"Tell you what. Let's do one more circuit. I promise not to drag it out, no matter who we meet, but you're allowed to linger as long as you like, anywhere you like."

"Wow. That's very generous."

"I'm feeling magnanimous." He nodded toward a waiter. "Pineapple juice? Champagne? Pastry?"

She held up her water. "All set."

He hugged her closer and they began the procession, and she truly did feel like a princess. Her free hand ended up around his back, and somewhere around a very large ice sculpture of Michelangelo's *David* that was a bit worse for wear, her head came to rest on his shoulder. There were a number of places she thought about stopping, because the odds of her seeing these people again were nil, but not even Michael Kors himself was enough to pull her out of the spell of being with Charlie, her one-night-only prince.

5

THE LIMO ARRIVED, AND THANK goodness Charlie knew the driver because all of the limos looked identical, except for the radical fringe who liked their Hummers and their Bentleys stretched and bedazzled. Chivalry wasn't dead, Bree was glad to see, as Charlie stood in the safety position blocking her as she got into the backseat. When he climbed in after, he pulled her close, his arm around her shoulders.

"That was amazing," she said, rubbing her hands together in an attempt to get warmer.

"It was. Everyone came out to play tonight."

"I'm still trying to get it in my head that it happened, that it wasn't a dream."

"Nope. A hell of a lot of the pictures and videos coming out of tonight are for *Naked New York*. I'll make sure you get copies, how's that?"

Bree looked up at him, astonished. "Really? Of everything?"

"Yep. On disk, so you can Photoshop whomever. Just do me a favor and don't publish them. That could get tricky."

"I won't, I swear it. Not the Photoshop part—I'm totally going to do that, and I'm going to save every last nickel until I can get a color printer, but I swear I won't publish. I wouldn't abuse the privilege."

"I'm not worried."

She couldn't stop staring at him. "How can you not be? You don't know me at all. I could be anyone. A competitor. I could work for Perez Hilton or Gawker, and then where would you be?"

"You don't, though. Because Rebecca likes you."

"She barely knows me, either."

"Rebecca has excellent instincts about people. You'll do well to stick with her. Don't tell her I said this, but she's very, very smart. The smartest one in the family, and we've got a couple of federal judges running around, in addition to a bunch of politicians."

"Speaking of, lately I've been seeing all these billboards for Andrew Winslow III. I didn't think of it before, but are you guys related?"

Charlie's expression turned sour. "And so it begins. He's a cousin. Not one I'm fond of. Although, I'm not fond of most of them. Rebecca is the exception."

Interesting, his distaste for his family. So different from her own experience. Sad, too. She didn't know what she'd do without her family's support. Best to get back to the relative he liked. "I'm enjoying the hell out of our friendship so far. Rebecca's ridiculously funny. And she knows the city the way I want to some day. All the little places and the secrets."

"Why New York?" he asked.

"The Chrysler Building started it," she said. "I love art deco, although when I first saw pictures of the building I didn't know what art deco was. Then I discovered fashion, then theater and what was available here, something incredible down every street. I fell for the city long before I stepped foot in it. And yes, thanks to Woody Allen, it came with a score by George Gershwin. I think I must have lived here before in another life. Not that I necessarily believe in reincarnation, but if it's real, then I was here. This is home."

"There's a heartbeat to this place that's either in sync with your rhythm or not. I notice its absence every time I travel. If you're one of the chosen, Manhattan becomes home base and every time you come back, it's as if you can finally breathe again. That's how it is for me, at least."

She smiled at him, as if they shared a secret handshake. She supposed they did. Then she leaned over, her head resting gently on his shoulder. "Thank you, Charlie. Tonight's been one for the books."

Charlie closed his eyes as he pulled her closer. He agreed about the night. It hadn't been easy to leave her while he worked, and when had that happened at one of these things? He couldn't recall.

Not that he didn't like the women he asked out—he did. He liked women of *all* sorts, but he had some strong preferences, he wasn't going to deny it. He wasn't just dating for his own amusement, after all. His image was part of the *Naked New York* brand, and so were the women he was seen with. Some were better than others, some he could talk to, some couldn't string two coherent sentences together, but to a woman they were a type.

Bree wasn't even close.

So far she'd surprised him in almost every respect, though, and as he'd plowed through the glitter, he'd tried to remember the last time surprise had been in the mix. Scandals were par for the course these days, scripted or not. Hell, scandals were the point, whether they were caused by celebrities or of his own creation. Parties were only excuses to be seen or heard or photographed. Everything was grist, and he was both the wheat and the miller. Surprises? Once in a blue moon.

He wanted to know more about the woman warming his side, which was also rare, at least in this circumstance. He'd always been interested in people. That's why he started the blog in the first place. Well, that and wanting to shove his parents' plans for him where the sun didn't shine. He wanted Bree's details. The minutiae of the life she'd given up to come here, who she hoped to become. Something to do with fashion, obviously. Was that dress of hers a new design? Meant to stand out? Charlie might be around high fashion far more than a normal person should be, but that didn't mean he was a member of the inner circle. As far as he could tell, Bree's dress was nice. It showed her shape, the look of her skin, her curves and the soft skin of her thighs. He liked it. But was it fashion? No idea.

On the other hand, maybe he didn't want to know more. He'd hardly be seeing her again, even if she and Rebecca were friends. Charlie's social calendar was a function of necessity, not desire, and however much he liked Bree…what the hell was her last name…she wasn't on the agenda. Couldn't be. Whatever had motivated Rebecca to set up this date, it wasn't to fix him up. He'd known that the moment he'd set eyes on the girl from Ohio. But he wasn't sorry for the time spent with her. She'd made his night.

She'd fairly sparkled with how the event had dazzled her. He had to give her credit; she'd handled herself beautifully in the face of many challenges, but even so, there was no hiding her excitement. It was likely she didn't realize how she came off. He had the feeling it might bother her to know that she lit up like a marquee every time she saw someone famous. The ideal fan, in truth. No squealing or flailing or "Oh, my Gods." Just that inner light, the spark in her eyes, the coy and charming way she bit her lower lip when it got to be too much.

He breathed her in, glad the perfumes of the night hadn't swallowed her whole. Another surprise came when he noticed he'd been petting her all during the drive home. Running his hand over her arm. By the time the car stopped, Bree was practically purring and from the look in her eyes, exhausted. Adrenaline drop, probably.

She sat up, looked at the building, then back at him. "So, this is good-night?"

Yes sat on the tip of his tongue. What he said was, "Only if you want it to be."

Her eyebrows lifted, as did the corners of her mouth, but a second later she hesitated and concern took over. "You don't have to. I mean, this was—"

"Do you have to work tomorrow?"

She nodded sadly.

He paused for a single beat. "Do you want to come up, anyway?"

BREE WONDERED IF SHE WAS reading the situation correctly. She inhaled sharply as she remembered his kiss, the way he'd touched her. If this were Ohio, she'd have known exactly what he wanted. In New York? She'd have to take a risk. "I would," she said, hoping she sounded far more confident than she felt. She was going up to his apartment. To his bedroom! Maybe!

Charlie helped her out of the limo, and slid his arm around her shoulders as she thanked the driver. They both nodded at the doorman, but nothing was said as she and Charlie crossed the lobby, his arm draping across her back, his touch warm.

They were quiet during the ride up the elevator. She fit at his side, tucked in neatly. It felt amazing having his arm around her, warming her with gentle friction. She studied him in the mirrored cab, but only got as far as his eyes, staring at hers in return.

They got out on eighteen and the doors opened to a small atrium and the entrance to his home. He pushed open the door and stood aside to let Bree walk in first.

Even after reading *Architectural Digest* for years, watching rich people's lives on reality television, she wasn't prepared for the beauty and elegance of the room she entered. "This is…" she said, heading straight to the windows that made up most of the far wall. The view was spectacular, Central Park in its winter glory, the lights of the city sparkling.

Bree wanted to check out his furniture, the gorgeous art deco design work of the black-and-white floor, the magnificent marble fireplace and the sheer novelty of so much space. But she couldn't stop staring at the city. Eighteen floors up, the breathtaking view covered too much territory to take in, not when there were so many other things to think about. She might or might not have another shot at it, though. What the hell, she could go to any high-rise in Manhattan to see a view, but Charlie was one time only.

Charlie spoke behind her. "Would you like something to drink?"

She turned to him, not sure of much, but she knew she was thirsty. "Tea? If you have any."

His hesitation made her think her request wasn't one

he got often. "I think so," he said. "Give me a minute. Make yourself comfortable."

Charlie dropped his coat on the back of a chair before he disappeared into the kitchen. The tiny glimpse she'd gotten through the swinging door showed a lot of stainless steel and what might have been the edge of a teak cabinet. Strange how when she'd mentioned her love of art deco he hadn't told her they shared the passion. Or maybe the apartment hadn't been his design choice?

The weird thing about her mental tangent into decorating wasn't the coincidence of their taste, but her reaction to Charlie. She was fascinated by him, beyond the obvious. Which begged the question: Would she have agreed to come up if he had been anyone else? Was she honestly as attracted to him as her hormones would have her believe, or was it the *idea* of Charlie Winslow that had her aching to strip him naked and do every naughty thing she could think of to him?

She opened her clutch and sneaked out Charlie's trading card. After a quick check to make sure he wouldn't catch her in the act, she turned the card to the back side.

* His favorite restaurant: *Grand Central Oyster Bar*
* Marry, Date or One-Night Stand: *One Night is his max, but it'll be a fabulous night!*
* His secret passion: *Down deep he's old-fashioned. I know, surprise, huh?*
* Watch out for: *The idiot is obsessed with his work. He needs a break.*
* The bottom line: *Have fun! Just be yourself!*

Bree grinned at the personalized responses Rebecca had inserted. This was one card that wasn't going back into the pile, that was for sure. No, this was Rebecca's gift to Bree, and Bree wasn't going to let her insecurity get in the way of the rest of the magical night.

She flipped the card back to his photo. Objectively, he was a good-looking man. It was well documented, how good-looking Charlie was, in magazines, television and online. But she felt completely drawn to him in a way that wasn't exclusively about looks.

She knew what that felt like. There had been times in college and here in New York that she'd liked a man's looks and just gone for it. Those times had been okay in a hedonistic way, not something she did often. But she had to consider why she was staying, assuming it wasn't just for tea. Was the quick beat of her heart a groupie thing or common, everyday lust or... Did it matter?

The answer was as instantaneous as it was physical. She wanted him in a way that was neither common nor everyday. She'd have wanted him even if he wasn't the King of Manhattan. He'd been a surprise. Nice. Captivating. He'd purposefully shared insider nuggets so she would feel less like an impostor sneaking into the palace. He'd come looking for her, and he'd laughed at her jokes, and he'd kept her warm. That kiss had been...

Well, she'd need to be on her toes tonight, that's all. If they did end up in bed, which was not a sure thing as there seemed to be a whole different world of signals and innuendos she wasn't aware of in this rarefied air of his, but if they did, she'd have to be careful.

How Charlie made her feel, *that* could be dangerous. That was the difference. The other guys, both of them, had been fun in that risky sort of exciting manner when you've taken all the safety precautions so you're not precisely scared, but he was new, and what if he was terrible in bed, or his penis was teeny tiny or he wanted to wear her underpants?

Charlie might have all of those issues, but that wasn't dangerous. The real fear was that she could *like* him. The kind of like that meant nothing but trouble. Liking a guy was not part of the five-year plan. In fact, it was the antithesis of the five-year plan, the one thing that could turn even this unbelievable stroke of magnificent luck into a disaster of epic proportions.

After tucking the card back inside her slim wallet, Bree rested her butt on the arm of a gorgeous white leather couch. She continued to wait, wondering what was taking him so long. As her gaze wandered across the cityscape, she reminded herself about Susan. They'd been college roommates their freshmen year, and they'd hit it off from day one. Susan had decided to go into politics. She'd taken prelaw, had already picked out the three schools she would apply to; in fact, it was Susan who'd shown Bree the wisdom and power of the five-year plan. Susan had been brilliant. Formidable memory along with a quick mind and a powerful presence. It was easy to think of her as a potential senator or even president.

And then Nick had come along.

Susan had fallen slowly. Incrementally. But fallen she had, so hard that it had knocked the plan right out of her. She'd gone on to law school, yes, but at UCLA because of Nick. Yale and Harvard had both come calling, but she'd been in love. Bree had been a bridesmaid at her wedding, and the two of them kept in touch on Facebook, but Susan had a baby now, and she was a stay-at-home mom, which was fine. Of course it was fine. But it wasn't the dream.

If it had only been Susan, Bree wouldn't have given

it too much thought. It wasn't, though. Almost every friend she'd had in high school and the early years of college, every female friend that is, had somehow, someway subverted their dreams because of love. Her experience might be a statistical anomaly, but it was a damn scary one.

Bree had nothing against relationships, but that was for later. She wouldn't even entertain the thought of marriage before thirty, and quite possibly longer than that. Forget a child in her twenties. She wasn't even sure she wanted to have a child at all. Not something she had to worry about at the moment, thank goodness, but liking Charlie? That was a distinct possibility.

Of course, his liking her back was highly improbable. On the level of her winning the lottery. Which was worse in some ways, because even though it was one night, and she had a hint of a crush on him, there was every reason to believe there might be sparks in the bedroom. It would be so very Bree to find herself enamored with Charlie, only to crumble in a fit of pining and lovelorn paralysis for however long it would take to get over it. That would also not be good for the plan.

This having-sex decision was more complicated than she'd thought. Thank goodness she hadn't given in to more champagne.

She wasn't wearing a watch, but Charlie really had been gone a long time. She pushed off the couch and went toward the kitchen, hoping nothing had gone wrong. Two steps later, the door swung open and Charlie came in carrying a silver tray. On it, he'd put a pot, an actual teapot, made of fine china decorated with flowers and vines. There were matching cups, two, and saucers, also two. A little cream pourer, a bowl of sugar lumps, tongs, *TONGS,* lemon slices, a strainer, and she had to get closer to see that the tins were actually different varieties of tea. She looked up at Charlie, and he looked back. It was a…moment.

Part of her wanted to laugh, but a bigger part of her wanted to know *what the hell?*

"Seems I have a tea service," he said, his voice low and wickedly deadpan. "I never knew that. I don't do a lot of cooking, and someone else put my kitchen together. But I thought, why not? I may never be asked for tea again."

"I see—oh, that one isn't tea. That's biscuits?"

"English shortbread cookies," he said. "Fresh, according to the package." He put the tray on the coffee table after she'd scurried to clear off some magazines. "My guess is that my housekeeper is the tea aficionado. She comes in three times a week, and I don't pay attention to her snacking habits. Makes sense, though. She stocks the fridge. The tea set looks like something my mother would own, and expect me to own."

"And here I was thinking a mug and a Lipton's tea bag. But this will do."

"It will, huh?"

Bree nodded. "So many different kinds," she said, busy investigating. There was chamomile, Earl Grey, Darjeeling and one she had never heard of called British Blend. She pointed to it. "Shall I make a pot?"

"Go for it."

She was very glad she'd used loose tea before as she poured the leaves into the hot water, then left it to steep. In her cup, she used the tongs to put in two lumps of sugar, poured in a hint of milk and waited nervously as she realized how close together they were on the couch.

This wasn't like having his arm around her at the

party or even sitting pressed up to him in the limo. A bedroom was now involved, only steps away.

She could take one of two approaches to the next minute: she could bring up the decor and keep wondering what was going to happen until he did something obvious, or she could put on her big girl panties and ask if they were going to share more than tea. "So," she said, "you like art deco."

Charlie glanced up at her, his own sugar lump tonged and hovering above his cup. "Yes. I do."

She barely heard him over the cursing in her head, which was frankly not very nice. She wasn't a wimp and hated to think she was a chicken, but the only way to prove she had cajones was to act like it. "Is the whole place art deco?" she asked, trying to be sexily coy, not creepily stiff. "Your bedroom, for example?"

She winced. She couldn't help it. A fifteen-year-old could have done better.

The sugar fell into the cup with a soft plunk and Charlie smiled. "Perhaps, after tea, you'd like to see it?"

Bree nodded, then busied herself with straining the leaves and pouring. She decided she'd said enough already, but Charlie didn't pitch in to fill the silence. He might have been watching her or gazing out the window; she didn't know because she didn't dare look up. It was enough to will her hands steady and her thoughts calm and composed. Something had happened in the past few seconds; maybe it was how his voice had lowered and how the husky murmur slid over her skin like a warm vibrant promise—she had no idea.

No, he was definitely zeroed in on her, she decided, as the weight of his stare seemed to change the very air around them. She could actually feel him watching, waiting, missing nothing. She set down the pot, picked up her cup and took a sip, barely tasting more than the warmth as the quiet stretched between them. The element of surreality, what with silver tongs and it being two in the morning, made time shimmer and slow. She drank again, the delicate cup insisting she raise her pinkie.

She finally glanced over and saw that Charlie was, in fact, staring. He also lifted his cup to his lips, drank silently, his hand large and his fingers long, his eyes never leaving her, never wavering.

She was acutely aware that he could have glanced down to the tops of her pushed-up breasts, to her barely covered thighs. If he had he would have noticed the intermittent tremors, the pink skin she felt sure was not just on her cheeks but the tips of her ears.

It was unbearably sexy, that stare, his dark eyes so large, unblinking. As if he could see more than she wanted him to.

As every second ticked by, the heat intensified, until she couldn't take it any longer. She blinked. "The tea's good," she said, surprised her voice was steady.

He swiped his bottom lip with the edge of his tongue; barely a swipe really, only enough for the light to catch on the moisture.

"Although I have no idea what makes it a British blend. It tastes like…tea."

He lowered his cup. "I've got a window in my bedroom," he said, his voice—still low and rumbly—moving through her like distant thunder. "I want to take your dress off slowly. Let it fall down your body. I've been wondering for hours what's underneath. I'm guessing black, maybe lace, maybe silk, but definitely black. You'll look incredible standing by that window with the lights of the city as your backdrop."

Bree almost dropped her cup, clumsy and awkward as a surge of wet heat flowed through her. She'd been so together, too. All calm and reasonable and thinking things through. And then he had to go and say *that*.

She was officially in another plane of existence because there was no one in the world as she knew it who could have said those words in that tone with that look in his eyes. If she hadn't known better, she would have thought there was someone sitting behind her, some model or actress or virtually anyone who wasn't Bree Kingston.

"Bree?" His smile was slow, controlled, while she hesitated.

God, why *was* she hesitating? A few more seconds and maybe she could get her legs in working order.

He stood and held out his hand for her. Heart beating flamenco style, head swirling in a cloud of lust and weirdness, she rose without spilling, tripping or making any unfortunate sounds.

Instead of pulling her closer, Charlie stepped into her personal space, then into her. His body touched her from chest to thigh, and he was warm and big and he smelled as if he'd just walked in a forest. Looking up was nothing new, but meeting his gaze so near, feeling his tea-sweet breath caress her lips, that was stunning. As he bent down, her eyes closed at the last possible second, and then, and then...

6

CHARLIE SHIFTED HIS BODY as he kissed her. He'd been getting hard for a while now, since he'd put down that ludicrous tea tray. Bree wasn't his type; there was no question about that, but she was something—

Something.

So small. Not thin, thin was ubiquitous, a thing to get over, not to enjoy. At least the kind of thin he was used to. Bree was diminutive, delicate. How he wanted to hold her completely in his arms, lift her from the floor and carry her off to his bed. More absurd than the tea service because there wasn't a romantic bone in his body and also not enough booze to let his imagination get away from him, and yet, his hands moved down her black dress—which had to go—to cup her hips, her bottom.

Instead of giving in to his urge, he walked backward, pulling her with him. He didn't need to look, not yet. It was a straight line to the hallway, where he would have to make sure to turn them, then another straight shot to his bedroom.

They kissed and walked in their odd shuffling gait. He touched wherever he could, mostly the parts that were bare, and warm, and pebbled with goose bumps. He hoped those were from him, not the temperature. Decided not to ask.

The bedroom was obscenely large for Manhattan, but the building was prewar and the place had been remodeled to make it expansive. He'd put in plush carpet for the pleasure of it, outrageously fine sheets, condoms and water bottles near the California king. Bree broke away from his kiss with a gasp. Not at the luxury of the room, she hadn't looked at it yet, but for breath. To give him a smile.

He nodded toward the wall, all windows, the electronic shades up and hidden to capture the view. "There," he said. "I want you there."

She turned. This gasp wasn't for air. "Oh, it's beautiful."

"It pales." He took her hand and guided her closer to the windows and kissed her again, sneaking his tongue between her lips as his fingers found the zipper pull. He heard nothing but breathing and blood flow, but he followed the zipper with his left hand on her bare back until he reached the end. He touched the strip of elastic that was the line of her thong. The touch was enough to pull him away from the gorgeous heat of her mouth. He needed to see.

The dress fell, puddling at her feet, and it was better than he'd imagined. The thong wasn't black, but red. Dark red, tiny. Seeing it against her pale flesh made his cock harder, his desire intense.

Odd, so odd, this reaction of his. She was pretty, she really was, but she wasn't architecturally beautiful. Perfectly proportioned, yet not so slender she didn't have curves and a little bit of a tummy that made him want to rest his head right there for a week. God, her breasts.

They were mouthwatering, with pale pink areolas and firm little nipples, puckered and waiting.

Bree stepped out of her dress, and oh, that was something. Her in nothing but a ruby thong and high heels. Stunning, delicious…for Christ's sake, the woman was two feet in front him, willing and eager.

He worked his clothes off in a controlled frenzy, flinging things away as he multitasked, toeing off his shoes and socks, moving closer to Bree as he unzipped, hissing as the silk of his boxer briefs brushed against the underside of his aching cock.

He kissed her again, but she was trembling and just chilly enough for him to bow to the nonsensical urge to scoop her up into his arms—she was a featherweight of soft flesh and hitching breaths—and dammit, he should have pulled the bedcovering down. She huffed a laugh as he stood her up, and together they got rid of the extra pillows and pulled down the duvet.

He waited, and when she sat and bent to take off her heels, he made a noise. It wasn't a squeak or a whimper, but it was close on both counts. Bree grinned, rose from the bed. There was a wicked sparkle in those lust-darkened eyes of hers, and when she turned around and went onto all fours on the mattress, Charlie made another noise, but this was a groan that came straight from his balls. She crawled across the bed, her hips swaying in invitation, giving him flashes of red between her thighs.

When she got to the second pillow, she made a show of lying down, grinning at him, flushed and breathing hard as she posed for him. Hands behind her, clutching the teak headboard slats, hair dark against the white pillowcase. Her legs came up, one canted over the other, like a pinup from the forties, like a siren, like a dream.

Miraculously, he didn't come right there and then. He made it onto the bed, took his time but he had to close his eyes before he touched her. Because, God.

When he licked a trail up the inside of her thigh, she trembled on his tongue.

BREE STOPPED BREATHING as Charlie's mouth inched up her thigh. The sexy pose wasn't like her, but then, she wasn't the same Bree tonight. Thank goodness her hands gripped the slats or she'd have floated straight up to the ceiling. She wanted to hurry him, his hot breath teasing her so near the creases where thigh met thong but not quite there.

He'd caught her left ankle in his hand, holding her leg aloft as his other hand smoothed up the front of her right thigh. She watched him, her excitement mounting, but the angle of her head was tricky to maintain with the firm pillow smooshed awkwardly under the top of her back. As much as she wanted to let her head loll back, her eyes close, let out the cry trapped in her throat, she couldn't do anything but stare at him, naked, crouched low on the bed between her knees. So she kept watching, urging him to move up, let that hot breath of his sneak under the silk, let his tongue follow.

Every inhale expanded her chest so her breasts, too small for her long erect nipples, came into her line of sight. When he looked up, he smiled at the same broken view, but from below. Okay, so maybe her breasts weren't *too* small. From how he groaned, never letting his tongue lift from her flesh, he seemed to like them. A lot.

Despite the groan, the stubborn man refused to *move.* "Charlie," she whined as she lifted her hips. What did he need, an engraved invitation?

His low chuckle dialed up her frustration.

"Patience," he whispered, his mouth moving closer to where she needed it. But instead of his tongue, he slipped his nose in that crease, nudging the thong over. He inhaled as if she were a bouquet of roses, and oh, God, he lowered her ankle as his teeth gripped silk. The tug was forceful, but not enough to snap the G-string panties, only to push things to the side, to let her feel a brush of cool air on her naked flesh.

When she let go of the slats, her hands ached. She was sure they were dented from the pressure, but she didn't care. It was necessary to touch him. She was shorter than any one of her friends, but the distance between the top of the bed and Charlie's body seemed to stretch on for miles. Yet she reached him with no strain, touched his dark, soft hair, her fingers tracing his temples.

He moaned, inches away from a different crease. Then that artful tongue of his started exploring and Bree's body arched with the shock of it.

The battle with the awkward pillow was lost in an instant. Her head lolled back, her eyes shut as he licked and sucked and flicked until she had one leg pressing down on his shoulder and a grip on his hair that had to hurt like a mother.

He didn't let up, not when she whimpered, not even when she turned his name into a pitiful plea.

She came with a jolt, another full-body arch and a cry that started low and ended so high only bats could hear it.

Charlie held her through the tremors, kissing his way up to her belly button, to her chest. Soft kisses, hard kisses, some wet and filthy, then chaste and sweet. His teeth scraped her skin, making her gasp, but the licks afterward soothed her into a sigh. When he reached her breasts, he settled in for a while. Bree quivered beneath him, every nibble and suck on her sensitive nipples sparking aftershocks.

She ran her hands across his shoulders as she whispered his name over and over, tugging him up, closer. But the obstinate bastard had other plans. He abandoned her nipple with a long swipe of his tongue and met her gaze, his eyes darker than ever. His lips were wet with her moisture, his smile three steps past sinful.

"You need to reach over there," he said, nodding at his bedside table. "Open that drawer."

"I do, huh?"

His smile widened and she felt his hand sneaking down her tummy. "If you wouldn't mind," he said, and she could have sworn his voice had lowered a full octave.

"Charlie, what are you doing?"

"I'm not finished being in you," he said. "So I'll just amuse myself until you think you might like more than fingers."

"Maybe I've got a thing for fingers."

"That's okay," he said. But he was pushing himself up to kneeling until she could see him. See his very hard, very ready cock.

The hand that wasn't petting her pussy, toying at the very edge of her lips, encircled his erection. It was a handful and he looked like he knew how to use it.

She swallowed and clenched her muscles as he squeezed up his length until just his glans peeked out, a drop of precome beading obscenely.

Bree hated to look away, but it couldn't be helped. She found the condom quickly, opened it with shaky fingers. He did the honors of putting on the rubber—

making a damn show of it—and then he laid himself over her, leaning on his elbow so she wouldn't be squished.

The kiss was salt and sex, his tongue giving her a preview of what was to come. Spreading her open, he rubbed up and down between her labia getting his bearings by feel. All the while, he watched her with dark, hooded eyes.

When he thrust, the cry she'd been holding in caromed off the walls, stole all her air.

Everything from then on was white heat and being filled. Raw and hard, every slap of flesh was followed by a desperate gasp from him, from her.

She came again. Squeezing him, pulling him closer, tighter. Then he froze, his face a mask of intense pleasure.

When he came back from the edge, he kissed her. More than the date, more than the tea, more than anything, the kiss turned everything sideways. Long, slow and deep, it wasn't a thank-you or showing off or like any other après-sex kiss she'd ever had. It was as real as the night sky, and it made her as dizzy as if she'd downed a magnum of champagne.

After, as she gathered in her stolen breath, he fell into a graceless heap beside her.

She still had her heels on.

When he forced himself out of the bed and into the bathroom, she closed her eyes, still dazed and confused. "Happy Valentine's Day, Bree," she said softly so he wouldn't hear. "Whoa."

It was six-forty. Charlie had looked at his alarm clock at six thirty-eight, then at Bree, still sleeping, still with him. All he'd been able to see was part of her bare shoulder and the back of her head. Now he was staring at the ceiling and having a panic attack.

He'd never had one before, but the way his heart was hammering in his chest had to be a sign. As a test, he turned his head to catch a glimpse of her. *Fuck.* What the hell had he done?

The last time he'd felt like this, not quite like this but the closest thing he could remember that had a similar vibe, was at fifteen. His first time. It was at Amy Johnson's house, in her twin canopy bed with her parents two doors down the hall. He'd been crazy about Amy, madly in whatever passes for love at fifteen. The sex had been horrible but he'd gotten off. He couldn't imagine how bad it had been for Amy. He'd felt like the stud king of the world, and even when he fell flat on his face escaping out her bedroom window, he'd considered the night a raging success.

He'd made sure his parents found one of the condoms from the box of Trojans. Their apoplectic fit at the inappropriateness of sex with a girl from that kind of family—she went to public school and her father was a dentist at a clinic—had been the most satisfying development in his life until age sixteen and a half, when he'd discovered the joys of older women and realized how much he had to learn.

Those lessons had been a downright pleasure.

But no one and nothing since Amy had recaptured the out-of-his-mind exhilaration of that maiden voyage. Until last night.

No matter what they'd done, Bree was definitely an innocent. Ah. Okay. Bree reminded him of Amy. Nothing to panic about. His breathing should return to normal soon. Last night had been a rerun of a great night. That's all. His reaction had nothing to do with the nice woman in his bed. He would give her coffee and cab fare, and that would be the end of it.

The sooner the better. She had to get to work, and so did he.

He stilled as she turned over and they touched. His hand, her thigh. It was warm, the place where they came together, and all the progress he'd made in the breathing department went to hell.

Why was he getting hard again? Shit.

He pictured her in that pose, her hands gripping the headboard, her nipples hard as little rocks and those heels. Jesus. She'd smelled like honey and tasted like the ocean, and he hadn't been that hard in years. He bit back a moan as he pictured her face when she'd come. And there was the problem in a nutshell. Or should he say in his nuts.

Forcing his mind to focus, he refused to acknowledge anything below the waist. If he'd been thinking with anything but his dick he would've sent her home last night. As soon as she'd asked for tea. Tea? Seriously? Then he'd made everything worse by getting down the goddamn silver. What was that about?

Screw his hard-on. This was ridiculous. He had work. Last night had been a favor for Rebecca, a nice surprise for him. No denying Bree was fantastic in bed, but that wasn't important. It didn't matter. He didn't need a great lay, he needed A-listers, women who would draw readers to the blogs, gossip fodder. He needed Mia Cavendish and her counterparts, the more photogenic and controversial, the better. He wanted to trend on Twitter, make the headlines on the *New York Post*'s Page Six. He needed ad revenue and infamy.

Bree could get him exactly none of that.

GOOD GOD ALMIGHTY, she was in *so much trouble.*

How was it possible that the best thing about her night as Cinderella had been a one-night stand with the King of Manhattan?

Not the limo, not Charlie's fame, not the stars or the dresses or meeting her design heroes. No. The best thing, the thing that would cripple her if she didn't get a grip *right this minute* was making…sex with Charlie.

She was no blushing virgin and she knew what happened between the sheets. She'd had bad sex and she'd had amazing sex and what had happened with Charlie wasn't even on the same scale.

Falling for Charlie was not acceptable.

She really needed to get out of bed because if he moved the hand against her thigh even a little bit, she couldn't be held accountable for her actions.

Where was her dress? By the window. Somehow, the room wasn't filled with light, which it should have been because the last time she'd looked, there'd been nothing but glass between them and Central Park. Yet, it wasn't dark, either. She hadn't opened her eyes, but there was some kind of pale gold thing happening behind her lids, so…

The lamp that had been on while they'd been…

She inhaled quietly, regrouping. It didn't matter what Charlie was doing. She was in control of her actions and her thoughts. She'd throw back the covers, get out of bed, pull up her dress, slip on her heels and go to the bathroom. She wouldn't have to look at him at all.

Crap. The back of his fingers brushed against her thigh. Just that quickly, her resolve vanished and her body tensed. Things were happening against her will. Nipples hardened. Kegel muscles contracted. Not to mention the thunder of her heart.

*It was one time, Kingston. One night. You had cham-
pagne. It was like being in a fairy tale. It's not real.
Things like this don't happen in the real world. It's over.
Stop being a moron and get out.*

After a silent count to three, she did it. Tossed
covers, pulled up dress, screw the zipper, picked up
shoes, darted to the bathroom, slammed the door,
breathed.

Cursed herself from here to Sunday because while
she was in the nice, safe bathroom, her purse with all
her stuff was in the living room.

She sighed and leaned on the door, barely restraining
herself from banging her head against the wood until
she passed out. Her makeup was already a disaster so
crying wasn't out of the question.

What were the odds he had a spare toothbrush in this
humongous room? The shower alone was bigger than
what she laughingly called a bedroom.

She could wash her face with whatever soap he had,
and rinse her mouth with something that would at least
hide the morning breath for a while. All she had to do
was be somewhat presentable for a cab ride home, then
she could start forgetting about Charlie as she hustled
to get ready for work.

Coffee. Coffee would help everything. No, *aspirin* and coffee. That's what she needed, and her world
would fit neatly back into place.

A knock on the bathroom door made her jump so
hard her dress nearly slipped all the way down to the
floor. "Um, busy," she said, yanking it up again.

"Yeah," Charlie said, and God, his voice rippled
through her like a slow fire. "I thought you might want
your pocketbook."

"Oh. Uh. Okay. Yes." She turned, holding up her

dress with one arm as she opened the door an inch. It wasn't quite enough. Another inch, then another, and finally her purse was inside. She snatched it as if it were connected to a mousetrap. "Thanks. Be out in a minute. Don't mind me."

Silence followed. Bree didn't know if he was there or not, but she didn't move. She pressed her ear against the door.

"Okay," he said, making her jump again. "I'll go make coffee."

"Great. Thanks. Sounds great." She winced at her stupid mouth, and reconsidered the whole banging her head against the door thing.

Finally, she turned around, resigned that there wasn't enough aspirin and coffee in the world.

"WHAT'S THIS?" BREE ASKED.

Charlie looked down at the hundred-dollar bill he was holding out to Bree. "Cab fare."

"A hundred? You think I live in Connecticut?"

"Wasn't sure. Look, I'm sorry I can't take you myself, but the blog..."

"It's fine. Really. I've got it," she said as she held up her to-go cup. "Thanks for the coffee."

"You're not going to be late for work?"

"Nope. Not if I get a move on."

She hadn't looked at him. Not once. At least, he didn't think so. He'd been avoiding looking at her, so there was no certainty, but it felt like she hadn't.

If nothing else had told him the night had been a colossal mistake, this morning's awkwardness would have. It was epic. Both of them stumbling, mumbling, embarrassed and basically acting like idiots. The problem was he couldn't tell why she was behaving like he had the plague. He'd thought the night had been great, and the sex had been fantastic. Too good.

Maybe that was just him, though.

Naw. It had been spectacular, and he knew what he was talking about. She was being weird for another reason. He'd like to blame the excessive cab fare move, but the weird dance had started when she'd first gotten out of bed.

She was making her way to the front door, although she didn't simply turn around and walk. She took a few steps back, checked behind her, then moved another couple of steps, and it made him want to kiss her.

Shit.

She had to go. Now.

He surged ahead of her to the door and opened it. "I'm sorry I can't see you—" He stopped before he repeated the whole sentence.

"Of course. And I have..." She was right in front of him now, looking up at him with those green eyes. "Thank you," she said. "It was the best night ever. I'll never forget you. It. The party. Doing...stuff."

Her cheeks had turned a really dark shade of pink, and yep, so did the tips of her ears. The urge to move a few inches, lower his lips to hers once more was stronger than he was prepared to admit.

"I had a great time, too," he said, his voice cracking on the end. "We should..." He stopped himself by biting his tongue. It hurt quite a bit. But he'd almost said they should do it again.

"Well, I'll be off. Down the elevator. To get a taxi." She stepped through the doorway sideways. Almost hiding behind her coffee, only spilling a little.

"Right. Bye."

"Bye."

He went to shut the door as she called for the elevator. Then stopped. It would be rude to shut the door. On the other hand, she looked desperate.

He split it down the middle. Left the door ajar, but walked away. To the kitchen. He didn't breathe until he heard the ding.

Holy crap.

7

BREE SAT IN HER CUBICLE, shuffling papers from one stack to the next. She'd been at the office for two hours and she hadn't accomplished a damn thing. Most of the morning had been spent rehashing last night, analyzing to death every single thing Charlie had done or said. Sneaking peeks at the picture she'd taken, of his trading card.

In the harsh fluorescent lights of BBDA, the events featuring Charlie seemed more like a dream than something that could have happened to her. But there was an ache in her body that wasn't a result of working out at the gym. She'd tensed her arms so hard gripping the headboard that her muscles had burned as she'd showered this morning, and there was that thumbprint bruise on her hip. Plus her memories, of course.

She had no business thinking about him. The night. Him. Really now. It was over. Done. A recollection that should bring her pleasure instead of this sense of loss. How could she have lost something she'd never had? Never could have?

God, the whole morning sucked. Her thoughts had been wild enough before she'd seen that he hadn't posted his blog yet. He should have. His routine was like Old Faithful, like atomic time. Instead, three other people had posted—one fashionista, one celeb tracker and one foodie.

So in addition to obsessing over the fact that sex had been no more than a part of the overall standard package rather than a romantically wonderful moment between the two of them, now she was pretty convinced that she had somehow jinxed Charlie. And she had a headache.

Surprisingly, Rebecca hadn't called yet, which was fine because Bree hadn't figured out how much she wanted to tell her and she wanted to be careful about that conversation, not dead on her feet. In fact, she seriously thought about sneaking in a nap today in place of lunch. She needed sleep more than food.

Her cell dinged and when she saw the name flash, she nearly choked. She clicked on the icon.

How are you feeling? CW

Bree stared at his initials, completely stunned. Why was he texting her? Good manners? Had she accidentally taken something from his apartment? She hit Reply then forced herself to think, not text, not yet.

This was silly. She shook her head as she used her thumbs.

Fine. Thanks.

You get to work okay? CW

On time and everything.

I'm glad. Also lunch? CW

What? Lunch? Was he asking her to lunch? Nope, no, that couldn't be right. Not after this morning. She stared at the gray panel of her cubicle for a moment, then looked once again at her message. She hadn't read it wrong. It simply made no sense.

Now her gaze lifted over the cubicle wall, but all she could see was the top of the heads passing by. There wasn't a single person at BBDA she could pull aside for advice. None of them knew about her date with Charlie. Or really anything about her except that she tended to keep to herself.

She quickly typed *BRB* letting him know she was away from her keyboard, and grabbed the landline. Screw not telling Rebecca about what happened. Bree needed help. Fast. She dialed, praying her friend would answer.

The second Bree heard "hello," she launched. "Last night was the most fabulous night in the history of earth, but this morning was completely weird and now he's…"

"Bree—"

"Oh, God, you're busy. Please don't be busy because I don't even— Wait. He's texting me now, and I don't know what to do."

"Texting you what?"

"He wants me to have lunch with him. Today."

Rebecca laughed. "Then go!"

"We both freaked out this morning. He offered me a hundred dollars."

"What?"

"For a taxi."

"Oh. Then I repeat. Go."

"But—"

"Trust me on this. I know him. Really well. Lunch is huge."

"Huge? Huge isn't good at all. It's over now, right? He doesn't do repeats, and I've got a plan, and it doesn't include liking anyone. Huge can't be the thing that comes next."

"Listen to me," Rebecca said, her tone one she surely must use when she was negotiating with billionaires or friends having panic attacks. "Go to lunch with Charlie. Eat food. Listen to what he has to say. You might be surprised. Then call me after."

Bree touched her hair and her face as her stomach flipped from excitement to dread and back again. Damn, she'd done almost nothing with her hair, and her makeup consisted of mascara. Period. She'd had barely enough time to shower and change, and then she'd had to scramble to make it to the office. "You'd better be right, Rebecca."

"I am. Good luck."

Bree hung up, then got her thumbs in position.

Where? When?

Bistro truck? CW

Um...

Mediterranean CW

Okay.

Sending map. U say when. CW

1?

C U there. CW

Her cell let her know the map had arrived, and the Bistro truck was only a block from her office. She typed the name into her search engine to check out the menu, wanting to be prepared and avoid anything messy. Figured she'd go with the phyllo-wrap veg and the Belgium fries, assuming she could eat anything. Even if meeting him turned out to be a horrible mistake, fries would soothe the wound.

After closing her phone, she stared at the paperwork she had to finish before noon, her vision blurring on the words. He wanted to see her again. Why? *Why?* And why was Rebecca so sure she should go?

New York was confusing.

CHARLIE STOOD ON A CEMENT bench on East 14th Street, searching the lunchtime crowds for Bree. Despite her little black dress last night, he remembered Rebecca's comment about Bree's affection for colors, so he zeroed in on anything that wasn't black clothes, which eliminated around seventy percent of the women. It helped that today was unseasonably warm, so that most of the coats were open.

He turned, not minding the stares he earned. This was Union Square at one in the afternoon. He did what worked. And work it did, because there she was. Her clothes hadn't caught his eye; her hair had, though. It was the same short pixie cut, but today she'd worn a slim pink ribbon complete with bow. It was ridiculous, and it made him grin like an idiot.

As she got closer, he forced his gaze down, not stopping on her face, not yet. No coat. Surprising, but not, because they were only a block from her office and she'd already proven she would rather freeze to death than ruin the ensemble. She'd need another winter in New York until she woke up and smelled the frostbite.

Today she had on a pink-and-green-checked long-sleeved button-down, which should have been ugly as sin, but wasn't. And a skirt, a little bitty one in a completely different shade of green. None of it had any business being on a single person at the same time. Even the flat matte gold shoes were wrong. And fantastic.

Her step faltered as he caught her eye. She smiled, one of those full-on middle American smiles that showed a whole lot of teeth. But as she started walking again that faltered, too. By the time he'd jumped down and met her on the sidewalk, she seemed worried. Or hungry. No. Worried.

"You all right?" he asked.

"Yes," she said, nodding. "Fine, thanks."

He wouldn't press now. First they needed to order. "Hungry?"

"Sure."

He grabbed her hand, and before they took a step toward the line at the big white truck, he kissed her cheek. He'd debated that move all the way over here. It seemed rude not to acknowledge their night together, yet he didn't want to emphasize that aspect of their acquaintance, despite the fact that the memory of her in his bed had been a constant low-grade fever since he'd opened his eyes this morning. It didn't surprise him that she stopped short and looked at him as if he were crazy. It didn't matter. He stood by the kiss decision.

Come on, how could he have resisted? One look at her with her pink bow and that small skirt...

Okay, shit, wrong turn. He breathed deeply the scent of fried foods and city buses, getting his bearings once more. They wouldn't be able to order for at least ten minutes, considering the length of the line, then there would be the food to deal with. Might as well dive in. He kept hold of her as he maneuvered himself close enough to talk without being overheard. "I have a proposition for you."

Her eyebrows rose.

"Last night, at the party, you were great."

"Thanks," she said, with just enough of a lift at the end to make it vaguely a question.

"I spent all morning trying to write the blog. So much time I ended up posting fillers from freelancers so people wouldn't get antsy."

"I know. I saw."

"Ah. Of course." He moved them up a half step in line. "Anyway, the thing was, you kept popping up in my first draft."

"I popped up?" She said it slowly, her forehead now furrowed in confusion.

He didn't normally confuse people. Piss them off, all the time, but clarity wasn't an issue. "I realized that I'd felt as if last night was my first time at Fashion Week. That didn't happen even when I did go for the first time. Seeing through your eyes was...different." He'd almost said exhilarating. True, but too much information. "That's what I wrote about. This morning."

"O...kay," she said.

He was not making his point. "I'm posting my blog late because I wanted to talk to you about it. I want to use your vision, for want of a better word, as the hook for the column. An innocent at Fashion Week. A new perspective."

"I'm not that innocent," she said, her tone brusque and bruised, as if he'd insulted her.

"You're new to the city. You're not jaded yet. Since *Naked New York* excels at jaded, I like the idea of approaching this series from another angle. I won't mock you. In fact, I won't use your name or image if you don't want me to. It'll be my impressions of your impressions. Which I've never done before, so you may or may not be fine with it."

"You already wrote the blog?"

He nodded. "Three different versions. One with you specifically, one with you obliquely, and one that focuses only on my impressions. I can send them to your phone now, if you want to read them."

"I would," she said. "Does it say that I...we..." She flinched briefly, then carried on. "You know, got together...at your place?"

"No. No, that's...no. This isn't about personal stuff. It's about the event. The party."

"Oh," she said, and this time it wasn't equivocal. "Send them, then."

He clicked the necessary buttons as a group of five in front of them suddenly dashed off, which moved him and Bree up to the food truck window. "What'll you have? I'll order while you read."

"Fries. Large."

"Nothing else?"

She thought for a moment, but couldn't imagine eating a whole sandwich. Not while her stomach was in knots. "Tea, two sugars."

He grinned. Couldn't help it. He still couldn't believe he'd actually served her tea on a silver platter. With tongs. Bizarre. But then, everything about last night had been.

He heard the sound of her receiving the documents on her phone, then he turned his attention to the guy behind the counter. He ordered, glanced at Bree, paid, looked again, then moved them to the waiting line where he out-and-out stared. He ignored everything but her body language, her expressions, the speed with which she read the screen. He learned absolutely nothing.

Turning so he could only see her in his peripheral vision, he reminded himself that whatever her response, it would be fine. Even if she went along with his whole scheme, it didn't mean anything. Not personally. This was a work thing. That's it. Maybe they'd have the opportunity to get together again, but that wasn't the point.

Even though the pink ribbon killed him. In fact, the pink ribbon *was* the point. None of the people he hung out with would have put that outfit on, not on a bet. It was an anti-Manhattan look. Those who attended Fashion Week were more afraid of not being cool than they were of being hit by a car. Bree's kind of unabashed adoration was straight from the heart with nothing expected in return.

Her point of view would ring true for the majority of his readers, many far more like her, young people who would never have a chance to go to a gala, never stand next to icons of fashion and film, never be able to afford a scarf from any of the designers, let alone a couture gown. The trick in this approach was the balance. There was a hint of sarcasm, because he was a sarcastic son of a bitch, but he didn't make fun of Bree. It was a fine line, a welcome challenge.

The whole concept could bomb, but he didn't think it would. He had good instincts about his readers, and this felt right.

She'd gripped an edge of her lower lip with a barely visible tooth, white and perfect. The urge to kiss her hit him again, only he didn't want her cheek, but her mouth. Ah, Christ, what was his problem? This was business.

"Hey, you. Blog guy. You gonna move up or what?"

The question had come from a beefy man with a pencil thin mustache. Charlie moved closer to the truck, gentling Bree along with a light touch to her forearm.

She looked at him as she closed her cell phone. Her cheeks blushed a pink that almost matched her ribbon. "Oh," she said.

That wasn't enough information. Out of an over-abundance of the need to appear cool at all times, he didn't push for more. He schooled his expression into one of disinterest, which was the only acceptable stance during a strictly business meeting.

Her head tilted a tad to the right. No blinks now, only a piercing gaze and "Why?"

"Why?" he repeated.

She nodded. "Your blog works perfectly as it is. Obviously. Your numbers are incredible. Why would you want to mess with the format?"

"Mixing things up isn't messing with the format. If it doesn't work, I'll find out quickly and drop the idea. It's not the first time I've tried something new, and it won't be the last."

BREE STARED AT CHARLIE. This lunch was even stranger than she'd expected. And not for any of the reasons she'd anticipated. It most definitely wasn't about the sex. Of course. Because that would have been crazy.

"Whatever your decision," he said. "I need to know quickly."

"Sure. Right. I understand." How could she have forgotten even for a second? From the moment Rebecca had shown her Charlie's trading card, she'd wondered what in the world a man like him would want with a girl like her. It had almost been a relief when she'd finally gotten last night that Rebecca had done her a favor, and in turn, he had done one for Rebecca. Why else would he have taken her out on Valentine's Day? Even so, it had not been a date. He'd been very clear about the fact that it was work. She doubted he was ever truly distracted from his business. That's how he'd become Charlie Winslow in the first place.

So he'd used her. Not maliciously, not at all. He'd found a way to parlay the favor, so good for him. He'd grabbed an opportunity, and by sheer luck, it might give her a spot on his blog. Other people would want to know who she was, how she'd scored a "date" with Charlie. She couldn't have asked for a better shot at her dreams. But she had to be smart about it. Especially smart, given that the girlie part of her brain seemed to want to turn this into a romance. Nothing wrong with romance, but there was a time and a place.

Now that she had leapfrogged into the big time, she had to be more clear than ever about what was in her best interest for the long term, and not be dazzled.

"Look—" he said.

"If you need to have an answer right this minute," she said, "it will have to be no."

Charlie stilled and that air of boredom he'd been wearing like a comfy jacket vanished. He seemed disappointed, but that undoubtedly had more to do with his plans being thwarted than not being able to work with her.

"Don't get me wrong," she said. "I liked it."

It occurred to her that she should have ordered more for lunch. She needed to appear as unaffected by Charlie as possible. "The approach is fresh for *NNY*. A good take on something done to death, and you managed to make me sound as if I'm not totally precious. Although…" She clicked on the most personal section of the blog he'd written and scrolled down a bit.

Here's what Bree said, but not in words:
1. Everyone is tall and beautiful and has better clothes than me. Anyone who looked in any way normal wasn't anyone. Example: Me.
2. People can be really rude, but at the same time, very lovely. Being with Charlie got me the last part. The first part was on the house.
3. Everyone has an iPhone/BlackBerry. And cameras are intrusive even if the whole point is getting your picture taken. Also? I'm really not in Ohio anymore.

"I'm really not in Ohio anymore?" Bree sighed. "Still. You did a nice job."

The way his lips parted, it was clear he hadn't expected her response, especially the way she'd said *nice*. Now if she could just keep it up. She'd imagined being the kind of woman who could go toe-to-toe with the biggest names in Manhattan, and now was her chance.

She'd been in Wonderland last night, and she wouldn't apologize for feeling like Alice. Charlie had captured that perfectly in his blog. But she was back on terra firma now. She knew the score, business was business, and if he was going to use her, then she wanted something in return.

Yes, he was *Charlie Winslow,* and her heart had been beating double time since his first text, but there was a larger picture here, and she'd be an idiot to let it slip through her fingers. Being linked to Charlie was cachet she couldn't ignore. "The blog would be better if you used my pictures. Used me."

"Would it?" A hint of a smile came and went. Good. They were both playing the same game. It was important for her to remember he had years of experience, whereas she had… She had chutzpah. It would have to be enough.

Charlie handed her a plate of fries and a cardboard cup of tea. He'd paid, which was appropriate. He'd called this meeting.

At the thought, she had a twinge of sadness, real regret, and dammit, she had to stop that. The sex had been sex. The two of them were about to talk turkey, and she couldn't afford to be sentimental, not for a moment. It had been great sex. The end. Her imagination could be a wonderful place, but it could hurt her, too.

Luckily, they scored most of a bench. The first Belgian fry was so good it made her moan, which made her blush, but only until she saw the spot of mayo on Charlie's chin. If she were the nice girl her parents had raised her to be, she'd tell him about it. But this was business, and him looking so very human helped.

"What's your concern?" Charlie asked.

"I'm really not as innocent as you've painted me. I understand that's the gimmick, which is fine, but I'd like to have some input. My bosses read *NNY,* our clients, too. It may only be one blog, but it'll have an impact on my career."

He took another bite of his burger, and instead of looking at his mouth, remembering what it had felt like against her own, she concentrated on the mayonnaise dotting his chin.

"I want more than one blog out of this," he said, after he'd swallowed.

Her gaze jumped to his eyes and for a sec she thought that maybe this wasn't *all* about business, but then she remembered.

8

"I'D LIKE TO MAKE THIS part one of a series," Charlie said, as if he was asking her for a fry. "Some of which would feature Fashion Week, but not all. Tonight there's a party at Chelsea Piers. I was hoping you would join me."

Bree didn't choke, but she did cough. Mostly to hide her astonishment, and get herself in check. "What do you mean by series?"

"Wednesday's open, but Thursday night is another Fashion Week party. Friday, there's a premiere. Have you heard about *Courtesan?*"

Had she heard about Courtesan? It was a major motion picture from a major studio starring major movie stars, and she'd wanted to see it since she'd caught the first ad. Inside, she jumped about five feet off the ground. For him, she nodded and took a sip of tea. "I have."

"I've got something else Saturday night but I'm not sure what. Either a perfume party or a book thing. Anyway, I'd need you, tentatively, through Saturday night. Maybe more, possibly less. It all depends on the number of hits, the comment activity. Could that work for you?"

To even pretend she had to think about it was useless. He'd know she was bluffing. "Scheduling wouldn't be the issue. I'd make it work, even if I have to get Rebecca to make my frozen lunches.

"That's the thing Rebecca does at St. Marks, right?"

"How we met."

"She's gonna love this." Now he didn't even try to hide his smile. It was the other Charlie, the charming cousin of her friend, the man who'd kissed her silly.

Bree cleared her throat before meeting his gaze. "What do you mean?"

"She's going to think the series was her idea. She'll be insufferable."

"Ah." Bree popped a fry as she fought against another pang. This one was even more foolish. She'd thought for a second there that Rebecca would love the fact that she and Charlie would continue seeing each other. Ridiculous.

But come on, this was better than dating. Sex for someone like Charlie lasted one night. He couldn't even fake interest the next morning. In the long run, what he was offering was more than her paltry dreams had imagined. He'd just shortened her five-year plan by half. "I still want input."

"It's my blog, Bree. People read it for my take."

"I don't want to come off looking like a fool."

"Is that how you read any of those articles?"

"No."

"We can draw something up, something we can both agree to. If the series works, it will be because people like my take on seeing my world through your eyes. It's in my best interest to make you relatable and sympathetic."

"Okay. But I think I would be even more relatable if I write some of the blogs myself."

He winced. "I don't know. My name brings the party to the yard. Sorry."

"Granted. Doesn't mean there can't be a sidebar. You've done that before."

Charlie used his napkin, wiping off the mayo by chance. After a longish pause, he nodded. "No guarantees. I'll read what you write, see how it works. I'll have my attorney draw up something to cover the rest of the week, but I'd like to post the blog I wrote today. What do you say?"

She knew she was taking a risk, not signing on the dotted line, but what the hell. Rebecca would have something to say if Charlie messed with her, but even more than that, Bree's gut told her to go for it. She held out her hand.

The shiver that ran through her body when they shook was strictly in response to the opportunity. Nothing more.

CHARLIE WALKED BREE TO HER office building, a giant among giants, blocking out most of the sky. It was windy in the street, and he put his arm around Bree's shoulders, pulling her close. He liked keeping her warm, liked the way her hair tickled his chin.

"Charlie?" She had to raise her voice as they walked, so he bent his head a little.

"Yes?"

"Assuming the paperwork is fine and we end up going to…things. What are we going as?"

"Uh, oh. Like last night. Together, but not a couple.

If someone asks, say we're friends. They'll all assume it's more, but that's not a bad thing. People like trying to figure things out, make connections, even if they're false. And gossip pays the bills."

She didn't speak, but she did slow her step.

"Bree?"

She stopped. Charlie turned to face her, not liking the troubled look she wore. "What's wrong?"

"Nothing. It's fine. I want to make sure we understand each other. If we do this, it's a business arrangement."

"Yeah." The way she stared at him didn't make sense. He was handing her a gift here. Sure, he was going to make money from the deal, but she would win, too. He should have asked her what she wanted. From her love of fashion, her work at the advertising agency, it wasn't hard to figure her area of interest, but it was sloppy of him not to get specific.

"I keep my business life and my personal life separate," she said.

It took him a beat too long to make the connection. Not because she was being unreasonable. On the contrary, she was being smart. He wasn't used to it, though. The women who came home with him didn't think of the sex as anything outside of the job. Neither had he, not since he'd started the blog, for God's sake. Bree was not from his world. That was the point.

In fact, she was a romantic. Not simply around the issue of sex, but about designers, New York, glamour, beauty, all of it. Too bad it wouldn't last.

Oddly, he didn't rush to agree with her. He'd assumed they'd sleep together. He'd wanted to. If the series got results, they were looking at a week, maybe two. That would be a long stretch to go without. Especially when she would be with him most every night. In the car, at his place.

"Charlie?"

"Right. No, you're right. Strictly professional. Good thinking."

Her smile wasn't very victorious. In fact, he was tempted to follow her as she backed away from him, just to see her better.

"I'm really late," she said, calling out now, against the wind. "Send me the contract, and I'll take a look at it. And the details about tonight. And, thanks," she said, but the word was carried away as she got swallowed by dozens of people all heading for the same entrance.

He lost her before she went inside. He knew BBDA took up four floors of the skyscraper, could picture where the copywriters sat. But he didn't go after her. He'd see her tonight. He pulled out his cell as he went to the corner to hail a cab. He needed to get the blog update done, call the attorney, make arrangements with the stylist.

After he told the cabbie his address, he looked back at Bree's building. No more nights like last night. Well, damn.

BETWEEN THE PHOTOGRAPHERS blinding her and the constant tweets, Bree barely had time to enjoy the party. It would have been overwhelming regardless. This event was much smaller. Maybe five hundred people?

Put on by one of the most sought-after design celebrities, it was being held at The Lighthouse in Chelsea Piers. The huge room had been decked out in Asian-themed splendor with floating lanterns, Zen gardens artfully placed between tables and paper dragons so large and beautifully decorated they were works of art.

Even the view of the Hudson River from the floor-to-ceiling windows stole her breath, and that was before she met a mind-boggling parade of fashion idols and A, B and C-list stars.

The good and bad news was that Charlie had been even more extraordinary, which she hadn't thought possible. He hadn't left her side, which was wonderful, but what got to her even more was how he'd introduced her to his people. And God, they really were *his people*. He made her sound as if she were the brightest new thing to hit the scene since Lady Gaga. It was totally over-the-top, but, and this went directly into the bad news category, it was totally to support the blog series. *She* wasn't important; the image was important, the mystique, the hip-by-association coupled with her "innocence" to make her a mini celebrity.

The plan was working though because after dinner—which was to die for, and God, how she'd wanted a doggie bag—she'd been approached, over and over.

Not that she hadn't realized before that celebrities were never what they appeared to be. They might feel as if they're old friends, having been on her favorite TV series, or in so many movies she knew. But who they were had no relationship to the person she'd created in her head.

She knew that, and she was fine with it. People had always had icons. It made them feel connected. Twitter, Facebook, *Naked New York,* Perez Hilton, E!, *People.* They were watercoolers, the center of invisible towns where neighbors gathered.

Being one of the chosen, knowing everyone she met, whether they were famous or seeking fame, had already made up a story about who she was, what Charlie saw in her, what would happen next, was bizarre in a way she couldn't have predicted. There was no preparation for this kind of exposure, and the strangeness of it was messing with her sense of time. One minute she was reeling from too many gazes centered on her, the next, she was standing beside a window staring out at the water without having any idea how she'd gotten there.

Charlie had helped. His hand on her arm was a steadying force, his presence, his introductions easing the way. But he was acclimated, and she was still gasping for oxygen.

It didn't help that each time, every time, his touch gave her a frisson of excitement that made her breathless once again. It was ridiculous. She should be over it by now. Knowing this was a business arrangement and nothing more didn't help. The disconnect between her brain and her desire worried her. It was as if she'd been given electric shocks all evening, each one immediately followed by a stab of regret.

"You ready?" he asked, his mouth so close to her ear she could feel his heat. It must have been a shout because the music was blaring all around them, but it felt like a caress.

She nodded, and he slipped his arm around her shoulders as they went from the steamy inside to the icy outdoors. Again, there were enough limos to fill a football field, but there were also dozens of valets, running off to find drivers in what must have been an underground madhouse.

"What did you think?" Charlie asked. "Better? Worse?"

"You tell me," she answered. "You were watching me like a hawk."

He studied her expression, and she was struck yet again by how much she liked his face. It really was absurd how outsize his eyes were. They weren't comic-book large or even unsettlingly out of proportion. They were definitely the first thing one noticed about him.

He raised one dramatic eyebrow. "You liked this one more, despite having to work. I think partly because you knew more about what to expect, and partly because you got to speak to some of your favorite designers."

She smiled even though his conclusion wasn't quite accurate. "You're dead-on. Is that a problem?"

"What do you mean?"

"I'm incrementally not as innocent. By Friday night, I'll be a stone-cold cynic."

Charlie laughed, and there were the lines on his face that made it impossible for her not to touch his jacket, touch him. Why lines? It's not as if they were deep grooves or anything close to it. He was in his early thirties, and they didn't make him look a minute older. Perhaps it was because lines of any kind, even laugh lines, were practically forbidden in this glamorous, youth-obsessed culture. She'd hate it if Charlie had Botoxed his out of existence. His lines made him seem genuine, made him seem attainable. *Seem* being the operative word.

"Trust me on this," he said. "While you're very savvy and not to be underestimated, you're nowhere close to jaded. It won't be as unbelievable to meet famous people in a week or two, but the thrill will still be there."

"Good." She wanted the thrill, at least as it pertained to celebrities. She could do with fewer thrills when it came to Charlie. "Sorry I'm making you leave so early. I imagine you close down these kinds of parties."

"Not at all. I stay until I have enough material, then

head home. I have to get up early to get the blog in on time."

"So the photographers send their pictures before they crash for the night?"

"Yep. I go through them in the morning. I also get the freelance pieces and gossip tidbits. I put together the blog, send everything to my assistant Naomi, and she does her thing until it's online by 10:00 a.m. If you've got a sidebar about tonight, I'll need it by nine."

She nodded, not wanting him to see how his mention of that aspect of the job terrified her. The words would be hers. Not an illusion, not a gimmick. She'd sink or swim based on talent. God, she needed to sit down.

"You okay?"

"I've been meaning to ask. The stylist? What are we aiming for here?" She looked down at the dress she'd worn, one she'd made back in college. It was a pretty green, a shade lighter than her eyes, and it was sleeveless with a purple-and-green bolero jacket. It would have been perfect for a night on the town with Rebecca and friends, but she was outclassed here by ten miles. She figured that was the point. Make her look like the hick she was.

"Ah. You're going to like this part. Glam to the max. Everything from shoes to gowns. The whole shebang, complete with makeup, hair, body airbrushing, everything."

"I don't understand," she said, unsure whether he was joking with her or not.

"Those sidebars? They should be about the entire experience. What it feels like to become a princess, to go to the ball. To be plucked out of obscurity and shot to the stars."

She blinked at him as people pushed forward to

get to their cars. Watched a smile bloom on his face. Wished like hell she could jump into his arms and hug him for yet another incredible surprise.

"And you get to keep all the swag."

She shoved him. Kind of hard. "Do not mess with me, Winslow. I will hurt you if you're lying."

"Not lying. Yours to keep."

Flashbulbs had been popping all night, but suddenly they were in her face, blinding her. Only for a moment, though, then they were gone, like a swarm of locusts with cameras. They'd done their job, however, and kept her from leaping into Charlie's arms.

It was the most diabolical torture. Give her all her dreams with one hand, steal her desire with the other. Rinse. Repeat.

"So, we discussed that you'll be meeting Sveta on Thursday, right? That you're off the hook for tomorrow?"

"Yep," she said, switching gears.

"You should sleep. You'll need it."

"I have to go make frozen lunches tomorrow night. Rebecca's going to be there."

"If I know her, she'll keep you up later than I have. The woman is a slave to details."

Before she hit the sack, she'd go through the pictures she'd taken. Those images were what she needed to focus on, not Charlie. Not his scent, not the resonance of his voice, not this wanting to be close to him.

By the time the series was finished, she'd be over her silly crush. Dammit, she would be.

9

"TASTE THIS AND TELL ME if you think it needs more salt." Rebecca stood back so that Lilly could try the soup.

She obliged and faked a cough.

"Funny." After elbowing her aside, Rebecca saw her cousin standing at the door of the St. Mark's basement kitchen. He wasn't looking at her, or, she imagined, for her. His gaze was on Bree.

Laughter still clung to the steam that swirled over the industrial stove. Rebecca was making a giant pot of split pea soup, Lilly was cooking a Texas chili and even with those pots and the 350° oven, the basement remained chilly. It wouldn't be for long, though, not if what she thought was going to happen happened.

It was difficult to look away from Charlie. He was as unguarded as she'd ever seen him. As an adult, at least. There was a keen awareness in his eyes, a concentration that spoke of a hunger that had nothing to do with pea soup.

One of his hands braced against the door frame, the other held papers. He looked elegant in his bespoke coat: dark navy, midcalf, styled perfectly. How Charlie it was.

The man knew what looked good on him, what he could get away with, and what would cause eyebrows to raise. Nothing was unintentional. Not online, in person, in a walk to the corner grocer. Seeing him blatantly wanting Bree was seeing him naked. Not that she had any personal experience with that, but she'd been with Charlie in family situations, private moments of grief, in trouble, in failure, in success, and this was new.

Rebecca grinned at her own brilliance. She was awesome. She'd known he would like Bree. And Bree would like him, but even Rebecca at her most conniving hadn't guessed they would have come so far so fast.

She'd have high-fived herself if she could have, for being just that clever. No one in the family believed Charlie would ever fall. He'd always have women, but never one woman. Not Charlie. His merry-go-round hadn't stopped spinning since puberty, and he got bored so quickly. Nothing could have suited her cousin quite as perfectly as this age of instant gratification. Charlie was born for it, breathed it, worked it. Everything lightning fast, and rest was for the weak and dull.

Bree wasn't dull in the least.

Rebecca turned to her friend. They'd played phone tag all day, then arrived at the kitchen as Lilly had come in, so all Rebecca knew was that Bree had gone with Charlie to a big fancy party last night, a heck of a second date, and she'd written a firsthand account of the party that had been in this morning's blog.

If that wasn't testimony to Rebecca's genius, she didn't know what was.

Things got really interesting when Bree shifted and sighted the man standing in the doorway.

If only the door had been closer to the prep area. It was difficult to know where to look. Bree now was a living demonstration of Modern Woman In Full Lust Mode. Her back straightened, her breath caught, showing off her chest in the most positive light possible. The thrift-store cashmere sweater she wore cupped her boobs perfectly, and Rebecca knew Charlie was having a little heart attack at the view.

Then there was the flush that swept across Bree's cheeks. Good lord, it couldn't have been more artfully painted by Renoir. Her eyes got wide and her lips parted and her pheromones were positively dripping.

The only sounds were the slow gurgle of thick simmering from the stove, the hiss of the radiator. Even Lilly, who'd come tonight for the company and the after-cooking drinks, had caught on that Something Was Happening.

Rebecca turned to Charlie again, and he'd dropped his hand, taking a single step inside the kitchen. He seemed to be fighting a smile. It would start to form at the corners of his lips, then flatten, but a second later the grin would start again.

Back to Bree, and it was like the slowest tennis match ever, the invisible ball staying well within the boundaries, the lobs back and forth languid and electric at the same time.

Rebecca's soup would burn in a minute if she didn't stir the pot. "Charlie," she said. "What's up?"

Rebecca almost laughed at how he jerked at her voice. And when she glanced at Bree, the blush had spread over her cheeks and down her neck, and there was a great deal of blinking.

"I came to show Bree her blog." He held up the papers as if proof had been required.

"Kind of hard for her to see it across the room."

Charlie's grin finally broke free as did his legs. He came inside, crossed the basement to Bree.

"That's Charlie Winslow," Lilly whispered, and Rebecca hadn't heard her approach. Luckily, no one saw Rebecca jump because everybody's gaze was on center stage. Even Lilly's.

"Yes, it is."

"Why is Charlie Winslow in the kitchen? With Bree?"

"Because she's seeing him."

"What?"

The word came out loud. Very loud. Loud enough that it halted the action.

Lilly smiled, gave a little wave. "Lilly Denton. Hey."

"Charlie Winslow," Charlie said. "Hey."

The moment passed. Rebecca dragged Lilly to the stove, Charlie went back to mooning at Bree.

"She's seeing him?" Lilly asked, her voice back down to a stage whisper. "Since when?"

"Not long."

"How do you know this?"

"Obviously you don't read his blog."

"I do, but I've been too busy the past few days." Lilly sneaked another peek. "That'll teach me for putting work first."

"Okay, it's not because of his blog, I know because Charlie's my cousin, and your chili is burning."

Both of them took up spoons, the industrial-size ones, and stirred like the witches in *Macbeth*. "Seriously, what the hell?" Lilly said.

"I set them up."

Lilly, who was something of a mystery to Rebecca, a friend in the making, but guarded, so very guarded, opened her mouth, then must have reconsidered. She did, however, step closer to Rebecca. "Explain. In detail, please. And remember, I have a large spoon in my hand, and I swear to God I'll use it if you keep being cryptic."

"I don't usually set people up," Rebecca replied. "Especially not Charlie because he's got hot-and-cold running women in his life, but he and Bree…they fit."

"Before the trading cards? During? Because if Charlie Winslow was a trading card then I want my money back."

"You didn't pay for anything."

"Rebecca."

"Right. He wasn't a card. Technically."

"I've been out with two trading cards. The first one was a wonderful guy, as long as you were willing to put up with his ardent love for his mother. The second guy's card said he wanted a relationship, but his actions were completely one-night stand."

"I know. My dates haven't been life shattering, either, although I hear Paulie met someone fantastic, and that Tess's one-night stand has turned into three."

"Which still doesn't explain Charlie Winslow," Lilly said, frowning.

"It's complicated, and we'll discuss it more when we go for drinks, but if I'm talking to you, my eavesdropping sucks, so let's keep stirring and shut the hell up."

CHARLIE SWALLOWED, WONDERING for the fiftieth time what he was doing in the basement of a church kitchen fumbling around like a teenager on his first date. Bree was reading the blog pages he'd printed out, and she was kind enough not to mention that he hadn't needed to come see her or print out the pages as the blog would be online first thing in the morning.

He'd asked her to do a little bio piece and tomorrow morning it would run. She'd already given a tease—her first sidebar about the Chelsea Piers party—and it could have ended right there. But blog hits had been up, and she'd gotten more than seven hundred comments on her column. Very encouraging.

So he'd moved forward. Tomorrow morning there would be more pictures of Bree, some from college days, one from here in New York in casual wear. He hoped it would start a dialogue.

His gaze went to Rebecca, whom he caught in mid-smirk, and he touched Bree's arm, interrupting her reading. "I'll be back in a few."

She nodded, and he went over to Rebecca. He smiled at her friend, then turned to his cousin. "A minute? Outside?"

Her eyes narrowed, but she put down her spoon and walked with him to the door. Once they were outside, she shivered at the cold, but didn't go back for her coat. "You can thank me now," she said. "And later. I accept gifts, too. The more expensive the better."

"We're not dating."

"I read *NNY,* you dope," she said.

"You read what I write on *NNY.* And evidently you haven't spoken to your friend since yesterday before lunch."

"That's true. We're going out after the meals are in the freezer."

As Charlie stuck his hands in his pockets, she grimaced. The bastard should have given her his coat. "Why did you set me up with her?" he asked.

"Why did you bring me out here to freeze to death?"

He rolled his eyes dramatically and took off his

coat with a sigh that would have done a Broadway diva proud.

She curled herself into the heavy wool coat, the lining as luxurious as the tailoring. "Because she's your type."

"No, she's not. She's not vaguely my type. Do you even know me?"

"Yeah. I do. And those skeletons you go out with every night are a joke. I imagine you can count the ones you actually like on one hand."

"It doesn't matter if I like them."

"You happen to be one of the only relatives I can stomach," she said, "but Charlie, it's time for you to move on. You're what, thirty-two?"

"Thirty-one."

"Over thirty. You've spent your entire working life giving your parents and our family the finger. It's enough. You need to start living for you, and stop giving them all the power."

He stared at her with his great big eyes, mouth open, as if the cold itself couldn't penetrate his shock. "What the fuck are you talking about, Rebecca?"

"*Naked New York.* Your blog. Not the others, not the legit blogs. Yours. The one that runs every aspect of your life. If you want to call it a life."

"I'm raking in millions."

"You already had millions. Look, I have to get back to the cooking. Do what you have to do, but think about it, okay? What it would be like if your evenings were full of things you actually wanted to do? If you went out with people you actually liked?"

"You're insane. The Winslow foundation has driven you around the bend."

"Yeah, well, maybe. Oh, and remember. Don't screw

with Bree, Charlie. She may want to play in the fashion big league, but she's a really decent person. She's not used to people like us. Tread lightly."

"I told you. We're not dating."

"The way you two look at each other? I give it three days. Four at the most."

"It's freezing, and I'm not listening to you anymore." He brushed past her, and she followed, wondering how such a smart, smart man could be such an idiot.

BREE LOOKED UP FROM the blog page as Charlie came toward her. He looked cold, and she saw why as Rebecca followed him. He'd offered his cousin his coat. Another nice thing, but not in the same league as what she had been reading. "You hardly changed anything," Bree said, when he stood in front of her.

"I didn't need to. You wrote a great piece."

"Wow." She flipped through the few pages, stopped at her New York picture. "Why didn't you say anything about my hair?"

"What?"

"It's all…wrong."

"You look gorgeous," he said. "It was difficult to choose which picture to use. Each one was great."

Okay, there was nice, and *too* nice.

Her suspicion must have shown because he touched her arm, making her look into his eyes. "I'm telling the truth."

She didn't speak for a while. Not that she didn't have a lot to say, but it sounded mushy in her head, inappropriate for what they were now. There were questions, too, about why he'd come in person, what it meant, and why on earth did she keep imagining longing in his gaze when longing couldn't be possible? "I have food in the oven," she said.

"Okay," he said, staring at her, waiting for…?

"After we put everything in containers and in the freezer, we're going for drinks."

"We?"

"Rebecca, Lilly, me. You?"

"That's a big crowd. Maybe we could whittle it down?"

It was tempting; of course she wanted to be alone with him, but that he'd even suggested it made her thoughts even more confused. "We've been missing each other, what with parties and appointments and things. I can understand if you'd rather not join us."

"No. I'd like to."

Well, damn. Why would he want to join them for drinks? Rebecca! That had to be the reason. "Good. You can help us put up the food. It'll go faster."

"Swell," he said, and she smiled at his put-upon tone. "Now that you know I make such great tea, you'll want me in the kitchen forever."

Bree's laugh stuttered, and a flush hit Charlie's face. She walked faster, so fast she had to look over her shoulder to say, "It won't kill you. I promise."

He'd come to a full stop. "I'm taking your word for it," he said, going for humorous, but not succeeding.

She made herself focus on food prep, and not the jumble in her head.

THE BAR WASN'T FLASHY. Most of the patrons were in business wear like Bree and her friends. She'd be willing to wager every last one of them was asking themselves what the hell Charlie Winslow was doing in a less-than-swanky pickup bar on a Wednesday night.

If she read him correctly, he didn't seem to mind. He had hailed their cab, insisted on paying for the short trip, then walked them inside as if this was the next stop on the Fashion Week tour.

The women in the place eyed him with undisguised hunger, the kind of looks that would make a statue blush, and all she could think was *I was with him the other night. Naked.*

She had to stop that *right now.*

They scored a booth in the back, and Charlie scooted in next to her, pressing against her from knee to shoulder. It would have been easier if he'd kept his coat on, but no, it was just him in his close-fitting white shirt, narrow black pants, and his hot body, clenching the muscles in his thighs and his biceps—

"Bree?"

"Hmm?"

"Drink?"

"Ah. Yes. Tequila Sunrise, please. Heavy on the sunrise."

"Got it." Charlie scooted out, and she instantly felt more relaxed. Jeez, didn't the man understand personal space?

Lilly leaned across the table the moment he walked away. The music wasn't deafening but it still made her have to shout. "Oh, my God, Bree, why didn't you tell me you were dating Charlie Winslow?"

"I'm not. Not really."

Lilly gave Rebecca a sharp look before she turned back to Bree. "I don't understand."

"The whole setup is a blog gimmick to get new readers. No big deal."

"Yeah," Lilly said slowly. "Tell it to someone who hasn't seen him look at you."

"Seriously, Lil? Come on. Would a guy like him honestly want to date a girl like me?"

"Yes!"

"Why wouldn't he?"

Bree blinked at her friends. Of course they would say that. What was the alternative? "Yeah, you're right. He could do so much better?" "Anyway," she said, waving off the both of them, "it's great. I get to go to Fashion Week parties, and he's publishing some of my pieces, which will make my bosses sit up and notice. I take a giant step up the ladder to success. Everybody wins, especially me."

Rebecca cleared her throat, and Bree reluctantly met her gaze. She did not seem pleased. "Why is Charlie here tonight?" she asked.

"Blog stuff."

"Since it's written for the internet, wouldn't it have been easier for him to, I don't know, send that stuff to you over the internet?"

Bree opened her mouth, but she had no answer.

EXCEPT FOR THAT WHOLE Psych 101 speech from Rebecca outside the church, Charlie had a great night. The food prep part he could have lived without, although no, that had been great, too. Rebecca was right about one thing—he hardly ever did normal stuff anymore. No grocery stores, no shopping in general, not when it was so easy to get everything delivered or picked up by his housekeeper.

He went to screenings or premieres, not movies. He was sent advance copies of books and films, invitations to parties from New York to Milan, Paris, London, Dubai, L.A. He didn't barhop, and tonight had been the first time in ages he'd had drinks with real people in a regular bar instead of with celebrities behind some form of velvet rope.

He'd liked everything from the music on the juke-box to the raucous laughter from the après-work crowd. He'd been reminded of the old days when he was just starting out with his first blog. The only part that wasn't great tonight had been at the end. Putting Bree in a taxi. Alone. And then hailing a cab for himself.

He consoled himself with the fact that tomorrow would be killer busy for his latest blog contributor. After a full eight hours at her day job, she'd be on the run with the stylist, then they had an art exhibit party to go to, which didn't begin until ten. She'd be lucky to get four hours sleep, and because he was a selfish bastard, he'd kept her out too late tonight.

He hadn't wanted it to end. But end it had, as all things did, and in a week, give or take, his time with Bree would be a memory. If it worked out, he'd use her for the odd column, and they'd run into each other at cocktail parties and openings. But he'd move on. That's what he did. What was for the best.

He thought again about what Rebecca had said. That his family felt slapped by what he did for a living was their problem, not his. He'd told them all the way back in high school that he wasn't going to fall into line. The idea of him going into politics had been ridiculous. They should have known that without him having to smear it in their faces. But they'd only seen what they wanted to see.

His answer might have appeared radical to anyone outside the family. Getting arrested in a public scandal his senior year in college was, he'd admit, a dramatic move. But Rebecca, of all people, should have under-stood. He'd done what was necessary. His success had been a matter of skill, planning and yes, luck. Why wouldn't he want to continue to thrive? It would have been nice to be with Bree. He couldn't deny the attraction. But she didn't fit. Not as anything except a temporary gimmick, a sidebar, a tweak on the blog.

And his bed. Good Christ, she'd fit there.

He stared at the window as the cab pulled up to his building. Life was about choices. Some tougher than others. Hell, she was just a girl. He'd learned long ago not to romanticize sex.

10

THE STYLIST, SVETA BREVDA, was tall and manic and thin as a whippet, and she wielded her opinions with an iron fist. The first stop—at *Dior!*—taught Bree to strip quickly, stand straight and keep her mouth shut.

She'd stopped being self-conscious about being naked by store seven. Didn't matter who was in the dressing room. Salespeople. Friends of salespeople, men, women.

For all she knew the pizza delivery guy was standing by the exit, nodding as he studied her slipping into a skintight dress with absolutely nothing beneath it as if he were picking out curtains. But the clothes were…

Bree had lost her adjectives. That's how fantastic the clothes were. And the accessories? Good Lord, she'd died and gone to heaven. Even though the shoes tortured her feet, she couldn't breathe in the two dresses that were honestly a size too small, and she was turned and bent and paraded around like a show pony, but the torture was totally worth it because she got to keep *everything.*

Even the bit where the silver-haired dresser from

Prada stuck his hand down her bodice and lifted her bare breasts. Now *there* was a blog entry.

All this done at the speed of a montage: cabs were hailed seconds before they stepped out doors, clothing selections were made preternaturally and perfectly, and she finally understood the worth of a good stylist.

The only thing missing was Charlie. She kept wanting to tell him things, to see his reaction, to feel his hand on the small of her back, but he was working, and she was, as well. Only this work made her feel like a model—despite the fact that every article of clothing had to be shortened—and like a prom queen. But mostly like someone had made a mistake that would be corrected momentarily.

Charlie wasn't the kind to make mistakes of this magnitude. Yet it would have been better if she could have talked to him. She'd texted in cabs—the only time she'd been able to—but he was in a meeting, so his response would have to wait.

CHARLIE HAD TO WORK TO KEEP his expression mild, to speak as if his parents dropping by wasn't something unwelcome and entirely too coincidental given his talk with Rebecca last night. He'd always liked Rebecca so much. She'd been his ally, his cover, his friend. Her betrayal hit hard and low. Shit.

"We're not here to take up much of your time, Charles," his father said, his gaze scrutinizing the living room. He—both his parents—were busy cataloging every change, the new lamps, the slate that had replaced the bricks around the fireplace. They'd only been to his place a few times over the years. He preferred meeting in neutral territory, although he went to family gatherings, typically one per year, wherever it was being held. He didn't shut his parents out completely.

"You've undoubtedly seen that Andrew is starting his campaign in earnest," his father said, his voice modulated and soft. That had been one of the earliest Winslow lessons. Speak softly. Make them *listen*. "We're very pleased with the endorsements he has now, but the committee is budgeting media advertising, and naturally, your blog group has come up."

So it hadn't been Rebecca. Charlie didn't acknowledge his father's remarks. Another lesson he'd learned at his father's knee. Never give anything away, not in expression, in tone, or in posture.

The Winslows were the quintessential image of subdued elegance. Nothing his parents wore was ostentatious, but everything was meticulously selected to evoke their status. The most expensive watches, Italian handcrafted shoes, tailoring from the finest hands in several countries.

His parents commanded respect, and made everyone who wasn't family feel small and insignificant. Polite to the extreme. They radiated power and privilege.

Christ, what they had tried to do to him. He was sure they wouldn't mention that it should have been his campaign, if only he'd not been so rebellious.

"We would very much like to utilize the family connection in the two most appropriate blogs, *Dollars* and *NYPolitic*."

"No," Charlie said. "I'm not going to promote the family agenda on my blogs. It's inappropriate, given I think Andrew would be a monumentally bad choice for the senate."

His phone buzzed again, and he took it out of his

pocket to find another text message from Bree. He couldn't read it now.

"We're not asking for a change of editorial direction or for you to give your personal endorsement," his mother said. "Simply space for featured ads. It would mean significant revenue."

He stared at his mother, knowing she was irked that he hadn't offered them drinks. It was only polite, the right thing to do, even for uninvited guests. In her home, nothing of the sort would have ever happened.

He smiled as he looked around. This was his home.

ON MADISON AVENUE, BREE and her posse stopped again, this time for shoes. Or maybe a bag, she wasn't quite sure. It didn't help that Sveta's accent—she was from Belarus—was nearly unintelligible. Bree mostly nodded and tried to keep up and not prostrate herself at the temples of fashion—Versace, Chanel, Anna Sui. Those were the kind of stores that only had a few items artfully displayed in minimalist snobbery. Where excellent champagne was served by stunning hostesses who knew every detail of the design and manufacture of the clothing on display. The music was always… interesting. Nothing you'd hear on Top Ten radio, because you could get *that* at the New Jersey malls.

The price tags made her hyperventilate. And even though the selections for her weren't the top-of-the-top-of-the-line, they were still extravagantly outlandish. Truly, she was in another world, someone else's life. Charlie's world. As she snapped another photograph of herself in a pair of heels that would likely cripple her after five steps, she reminded herself that she was a visitor. A tourist. Nothing more.

CHARLIE'S FATHER STOOD and even he couldn't control the way his rising blood pressure reddened his face. "Andrew is family, Charles. He's a Winslow. We've allowed you to set your own course, have your fun, but this is our legacy you're tampering with. I won't have it."

Charlie moved closer to the door, to the closet where he'd hung their coats. "Huh. It's good to know some things don't change. You continue to hold on to the ludicrous belief that you have any influence over me or my life. It's nice having our own traditions."

"Charles," his mother said, as affronted as his father, but less flushed. "That's enough. We are your parents."

He approached them and held out his mother's coat. "Thanks for dropping by. I hope you had a nice vacation in St. Barts."

She looked at his father who took both coats from Charlie. He didn't quite rip them out of his son's hands. But it was close.

"This will be remembered, Charles," his father said.

"I hope so." Charlie led them to the door. When it was closed behind them, he was still buzzing with anger. He needed to cool down, get Zen about the visit, about the message. He wished Bree were here.

He'd never mentioned his parents to Bree, hadn't asked about hers. They weren't friends. Yeah, he was comfortable with her. Okay, that didn't happen much anymore. But no. He wasn't going to talk to Bree about his parental issues. Jesus.

He pulled out his cell phone, and clicked on the earliest of her text messages. He was grinning by the time he got to his office.

FINALLY, THEY HAD MORE THAN enough clothing to get her through at least a week of parties. The most extravagant was the Marchesa gown for the Courtesan premiere. The evening dress, pinned to fit her body by a bevy of seamstresses, was so out of her league it hurt.

It was almost eight by the time the cab arrived at Charlie's. Sveta didn't need to announce herself. The staff at the front desk nodded respectfully as the doormen helped bring in bag upon bag upon box. Bree rested against the mirrored wall of the elevator, then took a few deep breaths before they entered Charlie's home. Her gaze went immediately to the hallway leading to his bedroom, and the reality of their new arrangement made her ache. Then he stepped into the atrium, and everything else became background noise.

He smiled widely when their eyes met. She shivered as he came closer, knowing he would touch her, and that she was allowed to touch him back, even in front of Sveta and the doormen. Such a mixed blessing. She could touch, but not have.

Bree didn't regret her decision about keeping the relationship out of the bedroom. It was the right decision, the mature way to go. It also completely sucked. "This is too much," she said, as she looked into Charlie's dark eyes. His hands went to her upper arms, and his palms ghosted across her skin down to her wrists and back up again. He kissed her, on the lips, yes, but the moment there was a hint of heat, he backed off. She wondered whom he'd kissed her for. Sveta? The rest of the team? Had to be.

"It's not," he said. "It's part of the gig."

"Charlie, I saw the price tags."

He smiled. "Most everything was free."

"Nothing's free. I know it's barter, but I'm not even famous."

"You will be."

"In a week? I doubt it."

He walked her farther into his apartment as Sveta led the doormen down a hallway, her heels clicking so quickly Bree wondered if it would be rude to suggest a switch to decaf. "You won't be on the cover of *People*," Charlie said, "but you're going to be known in the city, where it matters."

He paused, his palm warm on her skin. When he spoke again, his voice tightened along with his fingers. "You're with a Winslow now, and the Winslows are the very heart of power in this city, didn't you know?"

Bree stopped. She wasn't sure what was going on, but she felt uncomfortable. What had happened during his meeting? He'd brushed aside her questions, told her everything was fine, but that clearly wasn't the case.

"Each item of clothing is going to get a lot of mileage in the blogs," he said, letting her go. His voice had changed back to something less strident, more like Charlie. "In addition to your sidebars, I've got some fashion insiders who'll be plugging them for weeks to come. I guarantee there will be ready-to-wear versions in Macy's by April."

Bree forced a smile even though she knew he was upset, that this last speech was him getting his bearings again. But she had no right to ask him to be honest with her, to tell her a single thing about his private life. "I've already worked up a quick first draft of what it was like to be fitted by a big-league design team."

"Can't wait to see it."

Sveta's clicking heels announced her entry into the living room. "You come dress now."

Bree checked with Charlie.

"It's a media room. Used for these kind of things."

"You style up all your women?"

His lips parted, but Bree hurried to follow Sveta, not wanting to know his answer.

The room itself gave it away, though. There were mirrors, hair and makeup stations, clothing racks. A lot of those racks held men's clothes, but there were women's, as well, all stunning. In a shocking nod to propriety, there was a changing screen in a corner. There were also people. Five people—one of them was a photographer she'd seen at the Mercedes party. His assistant was fussing with lights. Off to the side were giant rolls of backdrops, like bolts of material, ready to be swung into place for any kind of photograph.

There was even a sewing machine in one corner, which Bree longed to check out. It was most probably the Ferrari of sewing machines and would make her so jealous she would weep for a week.

"Change," Sveta said, holding up the purple jacquard V-neck dress they'd picked up from the Victoria Beckham collection.

Bree obeyed, as if she'd dare do anything else. It was a matter of moments to slip out of her office wear into the magnificent cocktail dress, especially because her only undergarment was her own bargain basement thong. Beige on purpose.

The moment she stepped from behind the screen, she was covered in a smock, sat in a chair and set upon by far too many hands touching her hair, her face, her fingernails. The lights made everything more intense, hotter, scarier, and when someone said *open,* she opened her mouth, and someone else tugged her hair so she would bend her neck just so.

Her personal space had never been so invaded. The scent of many breaths and colognes went from cloying to unpleasantly sticky, and if this didn't end soon, she was going to have to do something, stop them somehow.

"Hey."

Charlie's voice cut through, and in two, three heartbeats, those things that had been touching her, brushes, fingers, nail file, eyelash curler, pulled back. Bree sighed with relief, saw that she was gripping the armrests of the makeup chair so tightly with her unpolished hand her knuckles were white.

She watched him in the mirror, felt his hand on her shoulder.

"I didn't even ask," he said. "Have you eaten anything today?"

"I had lunch."

"That was what, eight, nine hours ago?"

"About."

His eyes narrowed in the mirror and he turned to face Sveta. "How long until she's ready?"

"Five minutes. Nails on her left hand. Mascara. Lipstick."

"Hold off on the lipstick. Finish the rest. I imagine you haven't eaten, either. No, don't look at me like that, you have to eat something. There's a spread in the kitchen. Enough for everyone."

Before he looked back at Bree, he squeezed her shoulder and smiled. "It's not drippy stuff, but I'd keep the smock on, anyway. Just in case. We can talk about tonight's shindig while we eat."

She nodded. Calmly. Touched by his consideration. She hadn't realized her panic was hunger. Mostly hunger.

Unable to turn, she was still able to watch him as he went to the men's suit rack, grabbed one from the middle and went out. At the doorway, he turned and winked at her.

Before she could even smile, her hand was grabbed and the camera clicked and clicked and clicked.

THE BEST PART OF THE evening postshow was Bree, but even she hadn't been distracting enough to prevent Charlie from thinking about his parents. He'd put a call in to Rebecca, but it hadn't been returned, and his thoughts just kept circling back to this afternoon. How dare they think he was so spineless he'd cross the line into promoting the Winslow agenda on his blogs. God damn, that pissed him off.

He looked up as a Pyramid Club waiter came by with vodka shots. He'd done it again, let his attention wander, although at this point, there wasn't much more to be seen. Bree was standing against the black brick wall, looking beautiful in her purple dress, in her impossible heels, surrounded by newshounds and fame seekers.

He'd warned her it would happen. This morning's blog insured that Bree was now on the B-list, which could stand for "by association." He had the feeling it wouldn't take her long to stand on her own, though.

Most of the real celebs were huddled outside in the smoking zone, freezing their asses off while they dished about everyone inside, and he should go join them, at least for the few minutes he could put up with the fumes. But Bree was far more enticing.

She held up her glass of pineapple juice, but it was her shining smile that told him he'd made the right choice.

"You enjoying yourself?" he asked after he'd dodged drinks and drunks to get to her.

"Dizzy with it," she said. Shouted. The noise level at these things was going to make him deaf before he was forty.

"It's late. We should go soon."

"Whenever you like."

It wasn't actually that late. Just past midnight. But she had work in the morning, her sidebar to write. And he wanted some time with her where they weren't talking about who to schmooze, who to avoid. He held out his hand.

Cameras flashed as they went toward the exit. It wasn't a surprise that they were stopped several times, but it didn't take long to get the limo.

Once inside, he slid to the corner and waited for her to scoot next to him. Instead, she pressed up against the other door. "You okay?"

"Fine."

"You look…chilly."

"No," she said, tugging down her skirt, avoiding his eyes. "I'm good. Maybe you could call ahead to your building, give them an ETA for a taxi?"

"We'll take you home."

"I have my clothes at your place."

"You're wearing your clothes."

She looked at him. "Right. I forgot."

He moved closer to her, concerned. "What's going on, Bree?"

She folded her hands tightly in her lap. "I was going to ask you the same thing."

"What?"

"You've been jumpy all evening. I admit I haven't seen you at many events, but when I have you've seemed like the most relaxed person in the room. Not tonight. Actually, I felt as though something was off at your place."

He shifted away from her, not one hundred percent comfortable that there was someone else who could read him. There weren't many. Naomi. Rebecca. His college roommate. Charlie liked it that way. It had taken him a long time to cultivate the image he needed for the job, and Bree from Somewhere, Ohio, had already pierced his carefully crafted exterior in more ways than he cared to think about. He considered changing the subject for the rest of the ride home, making it clear she'd crossed a firm boundary.

Instead, he met her gaze. "My folks came by today."

She certainly looked startled by his admission. She wasn't the only one. He barely knew this woman. And yet… "They've wanted me to go into politics," he said. "Ever since I was in high school."

"Really?"

"The Winslows have had political influence throughout the generations. It was time to prepare a new senator from New York. Long-term planners, my family."

"Obviously you weren't enthused about the prospect?"

"No. I wasn't. It didn't matter to them, though. I was taught from an early age that we had an obligation to do public service. That our privileged life meant we had to dedicate ourselves to a larger cause, that what we wanted was immaterial. Which sounds great in theory, noble and philanthropic. But it had more to do with keeping the family in the top tier of society than philanthropy. My destiny was supposed to include law school, the *Harvard Law Review,* a prestigious firm, municipal office, a seat in congress, then the Senate. Carrying the standard of the Winslow heritage."

"Wow, I can't see you as a lawyer. Forget a politician."

His smile was wry. "And what, you've known me for a week? What does that tell you about my family?" He stared out the window for a beat. This true confession business felt as awkward as wearing someone else's clothes. "Not that I don't believe in public service, I do. I take that seriously." He faced her again. "What I didn't want was to live a lie."

"So you decided to become an internet mogul?"

"Sort of," he said, aware his automatic half grin said more than most of his conversations with women he'd slept with. "I didn't expect the blogs would become this big. Not complaining. I was in the right place at the right time. I wanted to be independent."

"It's worked. You are. And quite successfully."

"Yes. It's worked. It'll continue to work." He studied his hands. He was the one who was supposed to unsettle his companions. He was very good at it, and Bree wasn't even trying, so whatever this was, it wasn't a power game. No, he had opened another door for her. Game changers, these exceptions. It made him nervous.

Allowing his parents to rattle him was frankly embarrassing. They didn't for the most part. He'd just been caught off guard, that's all. But telling Bree about it? Jesus.

"So their visit was uncomfortable?"

He reached over and took Bree's hand in his. She was cold, dammit. "It was brief," he said. "I made my point. Have I said how beautiful you look tonight?"

She stared at him, at their hands, then back at him. "Yes, several times. Thank you."

"Am I making you uncomfortable?"

She sighed as she tugged her hand free. "It's not that I don't want to…"

He nodded, leaned back. Incredibly tired all of a sudden. Maybe he was coming down with something.

11

FRIDAY NIGHT CAME ALONG with a tux for the *Courtesan* premiere, and the only reason it was bearable was that Bree was in the media room getting prepped. He would check on her after he was dressed, although this time he'd made sure she'd eaten before Sveta snatched her away.

As he worked on his tie, he thought about the night ahead, pleased that she'd get to walk down a legit red carpet. A dream literally coming true, she'd told him.

The less sleep she got, he'd discovered, the more she revealed about herself. How when she was a little girl she would practice her Academy Award acceptance speech in front of the bathroom mirror, holding a bottle of shampoo or a hairbrush. She would very purposefully *not* thank whoever happened to be annoying her at the moment, which would sometimes be one of her siblings, a teacher, a friend or one of her parents.

It had made him laugh when they were slouched in the backseat of a limo, and it made him grin now. He could picture it so easily. He wondered if she'd always had short hair. Probably, given that she was so small. You wouldn't want to hide any of that face, not with hair, not with too much makeup. Sveta had turned out to be the perfect stylist for Bree. People were taking note.

Her blogs were getting heavy traffic. Unique hits were much higher than with most of his new contributors, which made sense because this approach was fresh. Charlie had never asked one of his companions to post.

Much of the chatter was about the two of them, naturally. Were they? Weren't they? There had been reports of Bree leaving in separate transportation at the end of an evening, and his place had acquired a few more paparazzi hoping to catch her doing the walk of shame in the morning. Speculation without confirmation was exactly what he'd been hoping for.

Bree had turned up on TMZ, PopSugar, Page Six, on almost every single one of his gossip feeds, as well as in the newspaper tabloids.

He slipped on his jacket, glad he'd chosen something so traditional. Beautifully cut, nothing radical. He wanted Bree to shine tonight. He had no idea what Sveta had chosen for her to wear, and he wondered how the stylist was going to top last night's look. Bree had knocked his socks off when she'd made her entrance.

Come to think of it, every time he saw her she got to him. Having her so close, and so damned untouchable probably had something to do with it. Okay, a little interest from his cock, not good for the cut of his suit. Not good in a number of ways. She was off-limits. The statistics didn't lie, and this new deal had increased *NNY*'s unique hits remarkably. It might kill him, but he'd keep to the script. Unfortunately, that meant touching. So much damn touching.

He checked his watch, made sure he had what he

needed in his pockets and then went into the living room. He glanced at the open door in the atrium and wondered why he hadn't taken Bree across to his office. It wasn't that far to the other side of the elevator. Then again, they hadn't had much time for anything but work.

He heard Sveta in the hallway, and swung around in anticipation of Bree's entrance. Damn. She did it again. Like a slap on the back of his head.

She was a vision. So much for not getting excited tonight. He would have to put his cock in a straitjacket to pull that off, and yeah, he did not need to be thinking that when she was walking toward him with a smile that made him forget how to breathe.

Her white-and-purple dress was a structured strapless design that looked like origami. It drew his gaze to her face, then right to the bare stretch of skin from her long neck down to the top of her bust. Her waist looked tiny, her legs slim yet curvy, and with that smile and those smoky eyes, no one would be able to look away.

Jewelry would have been redundant.

"Well?" she said, her shoulders moving in an almost-but not-quite shrug.

"You're gorgeous. You'll be the most beautiful woman on the red carpet."

Bree blushed, rolled her eyes. Charlie let her think he was talking her up.

He took her hands in his and kissed both cheeks. Very European. All business. Not close to what he wanted. He'd kissed her on the mouth that first night, when he'd barely known her, and now he ached to take her mouth again, to taste her, and not only her lips.

"We have a half hour before we go. Want a drink?"

"Just water," she said. "As excited as I am, I'm so

incredibly tired I'm afraid a sip of booze will have me passed out for the night."

"Can't have that." He nodded at the couch. "Sit. I'll bring you water, then take care of the rest of our group."

"Tell them again how wonderful they are, will you? I did, but I think they think I have to say it. I don't. They're magicians."

How could he not like her? She was the anticelebrity, the cure for New York cynicism, complete with authentic goose bumps and unabashed excitement. But even he could see she hadn't exaggerated about how tired she was. Not that anyone else would notice, but he'd been watching her for days, staring too frequently and too deeply. There was more makeup under her eyes tonight. He wondered if he should cancel tomorrow night's club opening. Bree had to work for a few hours tomorrow morning, but then she planned to sleep for the rest of the afternoon. He doubted that would be enough.

He fetched her water as she made herself comfortable, a feat in that dress, on the couch. Then he conveyed her compliments along with his own to the team and saw them to the door. The limo would be arriving any moment.

He could see Bree's dark hair over the edge of the couch, and he needed to remind her to bring her other shoes for when they got back in the limo. How women walked in those ridiculous heels...

Bree had rested on the leather sofa with one leg curled up under herself. The glass, now empty, tipped at a thirty-degree angle in her hand. She was sound asleep.

After carefully lifting the glass from her fingers, freezing for a moment when she made a little low-pitched sound, he touched her bare shoulder gently. "Bree? Bree, we have to leave now."

She mumbled something and adjusted the side of her face on the back cushion.

He hated that he had to disturb her. He brushed the back of his fingers across her cheek. "Bree," he said as he sat down next to her. He wanted to wake her, not scare her. "I know you're tired, but it's the premiere. Movie stars! Glamour! Lights, cameras, action!"

She tilted. Toward him. He repositioned himself quickly so she would land on the inside of his shoulder, not the bony edge. She slumped against him, the leg that had been tucked under now at a weird angle. While it looked ungainly and not very ladylike, it didn't seem uncomfortable.

It was too easy to shift himself, to wrap his arm around her back, to hold her close, to inhale the smell of her. Slumping turned to snuggling and he sighed as he gave his next move some consideration. Then, with his free hand he pulled out his cell. He had to call Naomi, as he wasn't adept at one-hand texting.

"You in the car?"

Ah, the voice. Car became cah, and he couldn't stop his grin. "No," he whispered.

"What?"

How she'd given that simple word such a swoop gave him equal parts joy and the willies. "We're not gonna make it. Danny can take my place. Catch him quickly, though, 'cause he's not going to be dressed for it."

"Why are you not going? Why are you whispering? Charlie, what have you done? It's something about the girl, isn't it?"

"Shhh," he said, although Naomi's voice over the cell

wasn't going to wake Bree. "She's under the weather. It'll be fine."

"How's it gonna be fine? You've got deadlines. You know how many comments you got today? Over twenty-five hundred. And you're taking sick leave? What the hell, Charlie?"

"It'll work out. Like always."

"Yeah, well, it's me you're talking to, sweetheart, and 'like always' my ass."

"Naomi. Call Danny. I'll send you the copy and photos in the morning."

He disconnected before she gave him additional grief, and put his cell down on the coffee table. Bree hadn't stirred an inch. She'd probably be mad at him for sending someone in their place, and he had no idea what he was going to do about tomorrow's blog pages, but there was no way in hell he was going to wake her. Not now.

She needed to rest. There would be other premieres. He'd spin the story to his advantage. In fact… He had the perfect angle. Take that, Naomi.

He'd have a story for tomorrow, but for tonight, he was keeping Bree to himself.

BREE HEARD A DOG BARK AND while it was a real dog barking, it was a dog once removed. A television dog. But she didn't open her eyes, not yet. She liked this place, the in-between where there was nothing at all unpleasant and no alarm was going to intrude. The subtle, woodsy scent of Charlie made her sigh and smile. He knew how to use cologne, not like some of the guys from work who showered in the stuff. There was always a hint of the man underneath with Charlie, and that was the best part.

She moved a bit, her head at a weird angle and it wasn't her pillow at all, and *oh.* It was dark, very dark. Charlie's window was right there, across from his coffee table and behind his big television. It was late. Wrong. All wrong.

"You're up."

She couldn't exactly see as some of her fake eyelashes were now sticking to her cheek, but she looked up in the general direction of Charlie's voice. "What's going on?" As nice as it felt to be pressed against his chest, she pushed off, up, until her feet were on the ground and she was sitting like a person. "What time is it?"

"A little past nine."

"Nine? p.m.? Oh, God, was the premiere called off? Did something bad happen? Is everyone okay?"

Charlie laughed as he rubbed his shoulder, the one she'd been nestled against. "Everything's fine."

"We were supposed to be at the theater at six."

"You were tired."

"I was…" She peeled the lashes off both eyes and settled them in her palm like two spiders. When she glanced back at Charlie he was still rubbing his arm, shaking it. She must have been sleeping on it the whole time. Hours. He'd undone his bow tie, the top button of his shirt, too. The apartment was darker than it had been because he hadn't turned on more lights. She'd slept through the red carpet. He'd let her. "I don't understand."

"I bet you're starving," he said, as he stood. "I know I am. How does Thai sound? Maybe some Tom Yum soup?"

"Wait." She raised her hand to stop him, but it was

the hand with the eyelashes. "Wait. Explain please. Why are we here? Why was I sleeping?"

"I told you." He turned to leave.

"No, you didn't." She stood up. She might be foggy headed and probably looked like hell, but she was going to get an answer. "Why didn't you wake me?"

He kept walking to the kitchen, his tux jacket swinging loose, and she thought of watching him take it off slowly, seeing those perfectly cut trousers fall.

Her heels clicked on the floor and made her wince with each step. Holy crap, these shoes were the instruments of the devil. Speaking of which, her dress, the architectural wonder of a dress, looked like a badly folded sheet. Sveta was going to kill her. "Charlie!"

He paused. Turned around. Smiled at her. "There'll be other premieres. I promise. I'll make it up to you."

"You don't skip things. You never do. I've read your blog every day forever, and you're always there. Even when you're not, you have a really good excuse. Like natural disasters. Not that your arm was trapped under a sleeping person. So what the hell?"

Charlie sighed. God, he really did look hot in that tux. "Take off your shoes. It hurts just looking at them." He kept walking to the kitchen, and she kept following, the pain in her feet making her blink.

"In fact," he said, not bothering to turn, "just get into something comfortable. We'll eat. You'll have a decent night's rest and so will I. We'll go back to the madness tomorrow."

They were in the kitchen proper and he'd flipped on the lights. It took her eyes a moment to adjust, to see he was holding a handful of delivery menus. Everything felt tilted sideways.

"Thai?" he asked. "Chinese? Pizza? Deli? There's

a terrific Indian place nearby that makes a hell of a chicken tikka masala."

Bree inhaled, noticed that she really needed to brush her teeth, and that she was still completely bewildered by everything that had happened since she woke up. "Whatever," she said, shrugging. "As long as it doesn't have cilantro, I'll like it. I'll be back."

She didn't make it to the media room before she took off the shoes. The dress came off in the hallway entrance. When she reached the racks of clothes, she'd already decided to wear one of the kimono robes because dammit, she wanted to be comfortable even if she did have to dress to go home later. Not a teeny short robe, either, because she didn't want him thinking she wanted *that*. They didn't do *that*. It had been decided.

Besides there was a particularly beautiful long black robe with a crane on the back that felt like heaven over her bare skin and covered her more than her dress had. She didn't even mind that it dragged on the floor. So what if she wasn't an Amazon? She was compact. Efficient. Far more comfortable in airplane seats.

The bathroom was next, and she debated keeping the makeup that had taken such time and effort to apply, but in the end it was just no. It took longer than it should have, but feeling clean and *herself* was worth it.

She looked once more in the mirror and stalled. It made no sense that Charlie hadn't shaken her awake. That they were here instead of Radio City Music Hall. The red carpet was long over now, of course, and that was the important part—not watching the movie. But there was an after party they could have attended.

It was highly unlikely that his excuse that she was "tired" was the real reason they'd stayed in. No, there had to be something bigger in play, but she was too fuzzy-headed to figure it out right now.

What she should do was get dressed, go home and go to sleep so that when she went into the office to-morrow to catch up on her real job, she might have an actual working brain cell or two.

On the other hand, a girl had to eat. That she got to eat with Charlie without a hundred people surround-ing them was extraordinary. Unprecedented. They'd been on the run for what felt like months instead of days, seeing each other in snatches and in the blinding light of flashbulbs. The only truly personal moments had been in his bed on Valentine's night—which she wasn't allowed to think about—and last night in the back of the limo. She'd thought about that conversa-tion all day. Not only about how different their worlds were, but how he'd opened up to her. It was as if she'd seen him naked again.

Screw it, she wanted to. Eat with him. Talk to him. Alone.

Her accelerated pulse and the rush of excitement that ran through her body merely thinking about what was next moved her out of the bathroom and into seeing dinner through. It was only her heart at risk, after all. And hadn't she admitted, to him of all people, that she *wanted* her heart broken by callous men who wore gor-geous suits?

12

CHARLIE GRINNED AGAIN. "So you're a black sheep, too?"

Bree swallowed her mouthful of noodles and took a sip of soda before she could answer him. "Oh, yeah. I was supposed to marry Eliot. My high school boyfriend. It was a thing. Big. Tons of teeth gnashing and hand wringing. Comfort food played a big role. In particular, fried chicken."

At the mention, they both ate for a bit in silence, which gave her time to go over what Charlie had told her about his struggles with his family. How was it possible for them not to be proud of his accomplishments? Maybe they were proud, but the family was crappy at communication. Rebecca had said that was an issue between her and her folks, and Charlie's parents were cut from the same cloth. But then again, Charlie was driven. He put the implementation of his goals above everything else. As did Bree. "You know what I can't figure?" she asked.

"What's that?"

"How come you're nice."

"Me? Nice?"

"Very much so. I expected you to be on the conceited side of horrible. You've been great."

He stared at her for a long moment. "Thanks. I'm glad you think so."

"Hmm," she said. "Interesting."

"What?"

"There was absolutely no agreement in that response. To be clear, I meant nice in an Ohio sense. It wasn't a dig."

"Well, then. I appreciate it even more. Nice can go either way around here."

"I gathered. How would you describe yourself?"

"Oh, that's a scary question."

"I'm not frightened."

"I'm not referring to you."

Bree grinned. "Come on. I'm already prejudiced in your favor."

"That's what's got me worried. I like that you think I'm nice."

"But…"

"I'm…focused. Extremely focused."

She ate a bit, trying on the word to see how it fit. "Is that all you are?"

His wince was extravagant for him. "Yeah, I'm pretty sure that's the whole deal."

"You're funny. That's not an opinion. That's fact. You make me laugh a lot."

"Hey, no fair talking about my looks."

"See? Cute. Very cute."

He put down the carton and picked up the beer, but he didn't drink. "What else?"

She almost teased him, but the look in his eyes stopped her. "You're thoughtful. You see who's around you and you don't take advantage of them. I'm not terribly experienced but I have the feeling that not every-one feeds the makeup and hair crew. Or even notices the building's security staff."

"That's manners."

Bree shook her head. "Nope. It goes beyond that. Most people in your position wouldn't give a damn about anyone around them. It would be easy to be hor-rible. Expected. But you don't need to be ruthless and evil to be a powerful presence because you're already a powerful presence. People get it. You don't have to shove their faces in it."

"I like that. Not sure I agree, but it's something to ponder. Of course, I don't want to completely disre-gard the whole ruthless and evil thing. That has a lot of appeal."

She gave a quick nod. "Yes. It does."

He drank some more, then reached for the rice con-tainer, but as he did so, he managed to move himself over until they were close enough to touch. The carton stayed in his hand as he leaned into her.

Bree held her breath. Warning bells went off in the distance, muted but not silent. "I should call for a taxi," she said. "Get home. Take advantage of the night off."

Charlie put the rice down, but his leg, his hip, his side were pressed warm against her. He smelled like spice and beer and her eyes closed as she inhaled. "I don't like beer. To drink. But I really like how it tastes when—"

He waited, not five inches between them, maybe not even three. "When...?"

"When I do this," she whispered right before their lips touched.

CHARLIE WANTED TO PULL her into his arms and kiss her until she cried uncle, but he held himself back, every muscle in his body on a hair trigger. Her lips were soft against his, brushing, teasing. Her breath came in gentle puffs, scented with galangal and heat, and no matter how fervently he thought *now, now, now,* he let her call it, let her make this decision. What the hell was wrong with him?

The whole night had been one bizarre thing after another. He didn't miss premieres. He didn't sit still for three goddamn hours just so he wouldn't disturb someone's sleep. He wasn't nice. Nice wasn't even a part of the equation, so what was happening? What was he doing?

A touch, fingers, small, cool, delicate on the back of his neck, and he became very aware of his cock. Not for the first time since they'd landed on the couch together. In another bid to make this the weirdest night ever, he'd found himself cycling through stages of hardness. From that first moment she'd leaned into him all sleepy and mumbling, he hadn't been completely soft. Not hard as a rock, either. Which was fine. He'd only touched himself the one time, and that was an adjustment. Even though this whole scenario was as close to an erotic dream as he'd ever had without sleeping.

She tugged his hair, pulled him closer, deepened the kiss. Little licks against his bottom lip, then the top, as if he were ice cream, a caramel apple. His cock filled, pressed against his fly. He should have taken off the tux, but it was too late to worry about that now. Not when she slipped her tongue inside and he tasted her for the first time since the party at Chelsea Piers.

Instantly he realized it was a mistake. A hormone driven error that would come back and bite him in the ass. He'd known better, but had he pulled away? Hell no.

He adjusted his head so they fit together better, then started his own exploration. He was not delicate or tentative. In fact, it was all he could do to stop himself from showing her just how ruthless he could be.

He opened his mouth and claimed her, sucked on her tongue, thrust with his own, and the sound she made, holy god...now he was getting the kind of hard that meant business. With determination and the endgame in sight, he pulled back. "Bedroom?" he asked. Hoped.

She blinked at him. Charlie realized he'd abandoned his beer and taken hold of her upper arms, the silk of the kimono warm beneath his fingers. She was virtually naked under that kimono; he knew that. He could see the push of her hard nipples against the silk. Maybe he'd been hit in the head or something, because this was not his style. This felt reckless, and he hadn't been reckless since his teens.

Her nod let him breathe again. He kissed her once more. It started out thankful and turned desperate with one slick of his tongue against hers.

They stood as they'd been sitting, his hands lifting her up, their mouths working together to remember, relearn, discover.

He had them halfway across the room before they had to take a real breath.

One of Bree's hands was in his hair, the other under his tuxedo jacket on the small of his back, as if they were doing some crazy waltz. "This is a bad idea," she said before she kissed his chin.

"Terrible. We decided." He captured her mouth again, amazed at how she let him guide her, backward, through the space. How, even with the height difference, the important parts matched, like her breasts against his chest and her lips within his reach. He only had to move a single muscle for her to react exactly as she needed to. It *was* a dance, not crazy, just theirs.

"Five years," she said, in a rush of air and half a moan.

"What's five years?" The hallway was coming, so they shifted slightly to the left.

"My plan." Her hand moved down right over his ass as they maneuvered the turn, and he pushed her back into the wall. Her "umph" made him swing her around as he stood straighter, the graceful equilibrium between them going down the drain.

"You okay?"

"Where's the damn bedroom?"

"Close," he said. Speeding them there would have been the smart move. He kissed her instead. The pull was too much, knowing he shouldn't, they shouldn't.

The hand that had been in his hair was now on his chest, rubbing in vague circles.

"What plan?" he said, his voice as husky as a pack-a-day smoker's. "To take over the world? To bring me to my knees? You don't need five years for either."

She laughed, stepped on his toe with her bare foot. It didn't hurt. "I'm going to be a cross between Tim Gunn and Tina Brown," she said, stumbling on the kimono.

If they didn't kill each other before they made it to the bedroom, it would be a miracle. "Good for you. You'll be great."

"Not if I can't say no to you."

He looked at her then, at her darkened eyes filled with a heat that could burn a house down. "You can."

She breathed in, then there was silence. Only his heartbeat loud in his ears.

"Please don't make me," she whispered.

A dark sound came out of his throat as he bent over

and lifted her into his arms. It was ridiculous, something he never did, would never do, but he'd had enough walking, enough of everything but stripping her bare, burying himself inside her for as long as he could, as deeply as he could.

"Charlie," she said, working her arm around his neck. "We're insane."

"I know." The door was there, right there, and it was open. He had her inside in a flash, over the bed in two, but he had to kiss her one more time before he let her go.

She pulled back from the kiss first, but she barely moved. Her breath brushed his face, soft panting, a faint-as-a-whisper tremor.

He lowered her slowly, head on the pillow, the shoulder of the kimono slipping down enough for him to see the crease where her arm pressed next to her side. It made his cock jerk and he wanted her so badly he didn't know what to do.

"It's my turn," she said.

"What?" He pulled his gaze from that patch of heretofore ordinary skin. "Your turn?"

Her normally very sweet smile and her big innocent eyes turned wicked as she looked him over. "Strip for me. Slowly."

He had to grin. She'd said the words like a crime boss, like a vixen. And then she shrugged that partially bared shoulder until the kimono… He could see the edge of her hardened nipple. Only the edge.

BREE BIT HER LOWER LIP hard as Charlie took off his jacket. He'd taken her at her word, so his movements were unhurried, but his technique? Bless his heart, he had no clue how to do a sexy striptease. He kept checking to make sure he wasn't going to trip and he tried to take both arms out of his sleeves at once and that made him cuss, and start again. She didn't want to laugh because, oh, God, he was trying so hard. Her whole body ached with how adorable he was, how the normally smooth, completely controlled internet mogul looked exactly like a seventeen-year-old virgin trying to impress the prom queen. They both relaxed when the jacket hit the floor. She wasn't about to put him through it again with his shirt and trousers.

"Come here," she said, patting the bed. "You needed a fedora for that move. Besides, you're too far away."

"Now look who's being nice," he said as he sat beside her.

Her fingers were working on his buttons. They looked fantastic—it was Armani, after all—but they were small and round and not easy with shaking fingers. By button three, she was tempted to rip the damn shirt open, but she could never abuse quality fashion like that. It would be like shooting Bambi.

Charlie ended up helping, and every time their fingers brushed she gasped. Couldn't help it. Now that he wasn't even trying, his unbuttoned shirt slid off his shoulders as if choreographed, and holy crap, he was half-naked, and so was she.

"This is going to be bad," she said, her perfectly painted fingernails trailing up his beautifully sculpted chest. Somehow, his muscles, his whole body, had been made to her specifications. Enough definition and muscle to be a gorgeous surprise, an ass to die for, and all of it belonging to the same Charlie who'd let her sleep, who made sure she ate, who'd given her a shot at her dreams. "It's everything I want," she went on, "and that never ends well." She finished the sentence with her lips on his chest.

His fingers smoothed through her hair, his inhalation loud in the quiet room. She kissed him again, moving over the warm flesh in front of her, sneaking her free hand to his slacks, only to realize she'd never get him naked like this. He couldn't have picked a more perfect tuxedo for the night. Stunning and sinfully elegant, and yet everything that kept the structure together—buttons, snaps, zippers—were as complicated as menswear could get. She wondered if somehow he'd found boxer briefs that needed a password to come off.

His fingers cupped her chin, and he lifted her up and away from his chest. "We can stop," he said. "I'll have to excuse myself for a few minutes, but we can stop right now."

She nodded, knowing it was the right thing to do, but when he sighed his disappointment, she grabbed for his hand to keep him from going. "There are too many things," she said.

"I'm not—"

"I keep thinking of all the things we didn't do that one time. How we wouldn't get another chance, and I'd never know..." She felt the blush and marveled at her absurd Midwestern shyness.

"Like what?" he asked, leaning over her more closely, his free hand moving to his difficult trousers.

She captured his index finger between her lips. Then she flicked the pad with her tongue before she sucked the digit into her mouth. She tasted him, fluttered her tongue against his flesh, made him understand.

His moan had her squeezing her legs together. She released his finger, but only so he could finish undressing. To say he was eager was an understatement, and he must have worn that tux often to be so adept, but she never blinked as the trousers hit the floor, followed by his sleek black blessedly uncomplicated briefs. Somewhere along the way, he'd toed off his socks, and there he stood. Oh, so hard. His cock painting a wet trail on his stomach as his chest rose and fell in harsh, quick pants.

"You thought about that?" he asked.

She nodded. Ran her hand up between the folds of the kimono, slowing as she traced her bared nipple. "I would really like it if you'd lie down. Soon."

His smile was as erotic as his erection, and both of them together made her squirm. He obliged, not without stealing a kiss that lasted a long, long time. Finally he was spread out next to her, and she could do whatever she liked. Taste, lick, nibble, tease.

She may have said it before, but this time she meant it. No more sex after this, because as she slipped off her panties on her way to straddling Charlie's hips, she realized that it wasn't exactly the smile or the erection or the meals or the clothes. It *was* everything she wanted. *He* was. Charlie. There was no use pretending, not anymore. This was no crush.

HE WAS GOING TO BURST into flames. There'd be nothing left but ash, and it would be worth it. Naked Bree straddling his waist was exactly the last view he wanted. The smile was a bonus, her bending over to kiss him more than a mortal man could take.

The kiss wasn't half as sweet as her grin. In fact, it was kind of a mess, full of tongue and teeth and saliva and his hips lifted her straight up off the bed it was so hot. Her hands on his chest steadied her, but before they had to break for the next breath, her fingers found his nipples. He loved nipple play, but the woman on top gave him two synchronized twitches that forced his head back, his eyes to widen then slam shut and he wasn't even going to try to explain the noise he made.

"This is fun," she said in the most wicked voice ever.

"You're killing me."

"Don't be such a baby. You can take it."

"I'm not used to this kind of insolence," he said, giving her his most imperious stare.

She raised her left eyebrow as she sat up. He only noticed she'd moved her hand around back when she gripped his cock.

He roared up again, thrusting his hips, her, everything, for more. Now. Please.

Then she pumped. Once.

He already knew she weighed next to nothing. He could simply lift her up, reseat her again in a more agreeable position. Because being inside her in the next ten seconds was the most important thing that would ever happen to him, ever, for his whole life, no exceptions.

When she let go he wanted to cry, and would have if he wasn't such a manly man.

Then she scooted back, lifting herself over his cock until she was settled on his thighs, and shit, the view, her bare-naked pussy spread obscenely exactly where he couldn't touch it.

One finger touched the base of his cock and she drew the finger up and up, and his back arched along with it. The crazy thing was, the whole time, he was looking at her, staring into her eyes, and she was laughing. Not out loud, not mean or taunting, just…delighted. Like a kid with the best toy ever. Jesus.

Her mouth opened in a big smile just before she bent over, and engulfed the head of his prick.

His shout came all the way from his balls, and it was everything he could do not to come right then and there.

Game on, he thought. Then he gave up thinking completely.

She had no idea how long she'd been on the edge, but it had to have been hours. It was torture, how he'd bring her right there to that place where she held her breath, where she trembled and moaned and prayed, only to pull her over into a quivering mess, and then rev her up again until she couldn't think straight, until she'd pulled the fitted sheet off its corners, until she'd begged herself hoarse.

He came twice.

She lost count.

13

HE COULDN'T POSSIBLY be getting hard again this quickly, especially after a doubleheader, but his body was giving it a hell of a try. Charlie couldn't remember the last time sex had been this...intense. If it ever had.

He liked sex and he liked women, and he had liked some of the women he'd had sex with very much, but this, with Bree, felt different somehow.

He kept staring at her, his pulse quickening as her breasts, the nipples still hard and very pink, rose and fell. While the flush that infused her face and chest was slowly fading, her skin, like his, still glistened with sweat. He needed to get up, get clean. Offer her water, see if she wanted a shower, see if she wanted to go home, although he doubted that. It was crazy late.

His other hand reached over and touched her arm. She turned her head and grinned at him. "That was. Wow."

He grinned back. "Well said."

"I'm surprised I'm speaking English. With real words and stuff."

He laughed, squeezed her arm. "I have to do things," he said.

"Well, you're on your own. I can't move."

He nodded, or at least he thought he nodded.

"Here's what I don't understand," she said.

"Only one thing?"

"Ha. No. I don't understand a gazillion things. Starting with what we were thinking. Not that I'm complaining, mind you. But we did decide not to do this."

"Yeah, well. I blame you."

"What? You can't blame me. It wasn't even my fault."

"It was so. You kissed me."

"You ordered an entire Thai restaurant for dinner."

"You were naked under the robe."

"I had on a thong."

He looked at her again and found she was already staring. "You fell asleep."

"You didn't wake me," she said, only not as quickly. The gleam of laughter fading from her eyes.

"You needed rest," he said, his voice low, soft.

She swallowed, then turned over a little. She wasn't facing him full on, but her body leaned toward him. "You could have gone by yourself."

Whatever he'd thought she was going to say, that wasn't it. Because she was right. He could have. He should have. He could have gone alone. Called any number of women he knew who could have been red carpet ready in a heartbeat if he'd wanted company.

"Why didn't you go alone, Charlie?" she asked.

He pounced on the first answer that came to him. "I didn't want to wake you."

Bree's eyebrows lowered. If she was trying to figure out the hidden meaning in his words, she'd be at it for a long while because there was no meaning. No answer. No explanation. It hadn't occurred to him. Not once in three hours had he entertained the thought of leaving her to sleep so he could do his job.

Shit.

He let go of her arm, flung off his sheet then practically flew off the bed. Naked and really wishing he wasn't, he turned to Bree. "You want some water?"

She blinked, then nodded. "Sure. Thanks."

He got her a bottle from the mini fridge in his closet. When she took it, he headed for the bathroom. After he'd closed the door behind him, he realized he should have said something. Nothing important, just the typical, "Be back in a minute," or something equally mundane. According to Bree, he was supposed to be nice. What he was, in fact, was panicked.

He busied himself with cleaning up, but his thoughts were as scattered as shattered glass. He kept trolling for reasons, for a string of logic that would explain why he was standing in his bathroom washing the come off his dick when he should have been in his office finishing up his notes on the movie premiere and planning his morning blog. Alone. With no Bree in his bed or even in his apartment.

Nothing. It may not have been his idea to stop the sex when they agreed to work together, but he'd agreed. It only made sense. They'd had their one night, and even that had been questionable. It was completely out of character for him to change the rules like this. Something must be wrong with him.

He finished, barely remembering to turn off the spigot, as it occurred to him that because of the blog experiment, he'd been spending almost every night with Bree, which was unusual as hell, and not sleeping with anyone else, which was also bizarre, so, of course, he was off balance.

Okay, so he'd gone without having sex for longer than a week before and he hadn't done anything as stupid as ditch work, but the thing was, even during dry spells, he'd gone out with a variety of women. His batting average, despite the impression he cultivated, was nowhere near one hundred percent. There'd been extended stretches he'd gone without anything but his own hand. But he'd never gone any length of time accompanying the same woman to different events.

He snorted as he grabbed his towel. No cause for alarm. It was probably for the best if he didn't make a habit of this, of Bree, because that could get messy.

He could stop seeing her altogether. Fashion Week was moving on to London. He wasn't covering the show there, but neither was he covering the events at Lincoln Center. Tonight's premiere was only tangentially related, and after the club opening tomorrow night and the perfume party Monday, the town and the blog would move on. There was nothing in the contract that stipulated their working relationship would stop at the end of Fashion Week, although it had been mentioned. It would be simple, a nice, clean break.

Instead of the rush of relief he expected, Charlie paused again, his hand partway to the knob. He opened the door slowly, cautiously, unsure why.

She was in his bed. Sitting up, in fact, her side to him while she faced the window. If someone had been outside looking in, they would have seen her, backlit like a painting. They'd have seen him, too, which should have prompted him to shut the light, if not the door, because he was naked.

But so was Bree. She was naked and lit from behind, and he knew she could see his reflection in the window as he stared at her, as intrigued by the shadows as he was by what the light revealed. His gaze moved down the length of her back to the pillow at the base of her spine. He could see the proof of his fingers in her hair, the dark mark he'd made at the junction of her neck and shoulder. The soft roundness of her breast as it peeked out from under her arm—a suggestion, nothing more. It made him swallow, it made the base of his cock tighten and interest curl deep in his body.

He hated to do it, but he had to turn off the light behind him. The darkness wasn't complete because he'd thought of moments like these when this room had been redesigned. He was a visual man, and had no trouble sleeping when the space was less than inky black.

His image was still reflected, though not as clearly, but she could see him approach the bed, raise his arm, put his hand on her warm shoulder. "Stay?" he asked, his voice as low as the lights.

"I need to be up by eight. Well, eight-ish. I have to go to work in the morning."

"We can do that."

Finally, Bree turned to meet his gaze. "I was so sure you were going to ask me to leave."

"I thought about it."

She nodded.

"But it's late," he said. "And I want you here."

A barely there smile curved her lush lips. "Just this once."

He nodded. "Yeah."

"Good. Fine." She shifted, dislodging his hand. "I need to…" She nodded at the restroom.

He watched her small, perfect body as she climbed out of bed. She didn't reach for the robe, which was a surprise. But she was always surprising him.

The door closed before she turned on the light, and

he felt cheated. This was an irresponsible thing he was doing. Maybe that was the point.

IT WASN'T HER ALARM CLOCK that woke her at a quarter to seven. She wasn't sure what had. It took Bree a moment to remember where she was, and to see she was alone. She hadn't realized she'd wanted to wake up next to him.

The bathroom door was open, no sounds, no lights. She wondered if Charlie was in the apartment at all. It was only seven, so she could technically sleep for another hour or so, but that wasn't going to happen. A shower was, however, but first, she'd have to go fetch her bag, her clothes, shoes. Sadly, she hadn't packed her overnight kit. There weren't supposed to be any overnights. Lesson learned.

She grabbed the kimono and opened the bedroom door. It was quiet and chilly, or maybe the chilly was because she was hurrying across long sections of floor in bare feet. The sheer space of this apartment boggled the mind. She pictured her bedroom/closet and how doing anything was a logistical nightmare. The sewing machine couldn't be up while the bed was; the drawers had to be closed to get the sheets, to get anything on hangers. Most everything else was stored in her suitcases, which weren't particularly big or handy. And here she was darting the length of a football field to grab her bag before she rounded the couch to dash to the media room, never once hearing or seeing the master of the house.

She looked at her work dress and it made her sad. It was her own, of course. Not that it mattered. It was a Saturday morning, hardly anyone would be at her office and whoever was probably wouldn't remember she'd worn the same clothes two days in a row. She couldn't believe she had to go in at all, but between the shopping, the preparations, the parties and writing the blogs, she'd been neglecting her day job. God forbid she got fired. She was beyond lucky to have any kind of job, let alone a great one. At least she'd slept more last night than she had all last week. Which said volumes about how little sleep she'd been getting.

Tempted almost to the breaking point, she left the green DKNY dress that was calling her name on the hanger and fetched the blue shirtdress she'd made in college.

She debated using the en suite bathroom here, or going back to the bedroom. Staying here was too much like work, and she was off until tonight.

She kept her eyes peeled for him, surprised when he wasn't in the bedroom. Maybe not so much surprised as disappointed. Anyway, his shower was an otherworldly experience especially since the water pressure in her building was more or less random spitting. Even so, she didn't linger.

Fresh panties were an issue. She didn't have any, if there were some in the media room, she didn't want to know about it. She'd go without, but in this city? That wasn't a smart move.

What the hell. She went back into Charlie's empty bedroom. Second drawer in, she found what she was looking for. A nice pair of black silk boxer briefs. She'd replace them later.

Once dressed, she checked the mirror carefully, making sure no one would see her secret. It was kind of sexy, wearing something so personal of his. She might even tell him.

Then it was on to patching her makeup and fixing

her hair. It wasn't going to win her any beauty contests, but she'd pass. She left the kimono on the bed and went in search of her host. Or at the very least, a note.

She discovered that Charlie's apartment took up the entire floor. The elevator was situated in an atrium. His office took up most of the previously undiscovered country.

And there he was. Sitting in a giant room with enough computers to launch the shuttle. He wore jeans, which she hadn't even known he owned, and a scrumptious V-neck sweater. He made quite the picture, and not because he was so, so pretty—although that didn't hurt—but because he was in his element. The difference was written in his posture as he typed on his computer, as he sailed across the floor in his chair. She couldn't look away.

When he was at parties, even in the limo before parties, or when he was working with his crew inside the media room, there was never a moment when Bree wasn't aware that Charlie was watching. No. Overseeing. It wasn't super obvious, but she'd felt it, and on a couple of occasions she'd seen others notice. He was always one step removed, above it all.

That was one of the things that made even A-list celebs want his attention. He never gave too much of himself. He held back a small but vital part, the part that judged, evaluated. He was completely charming to everyone, so there was no hint, no clue. His real thoughts and opinions would show up in the next blog, or even worse, wouldn't show up at all.

But he was completely present in his big office. The difference in his attitude couldn't have been clearer. She'd been with this Charlie only twice before—in bed.

She shivered at the memories, still hardly believing any of it had been real.

He hadn't noticed her yet. She wasn't even in the room, just peeking in from the doorway. Bree wondered if it might be better to leave now. He was so wrapped up in the work, he wouldn't care. She shouldn't. Only an idiot would make more of last night than what it was. Tension relief. Nothing personal.

Except for the naked part and the kissing and how she'd felt when he was holding her.

Last night she'd had every ounce of Charlie. His body, his attention, his focus. It had felt like being plugged into the mainframe. Every touch electric and unique—

"You're being ridiculous," Charlie said.

Bree froze, held her breath. His back was to her, how could he—

"Naomi, stop. Just stop right there."

He was on the phone. Not a mind reader.

"Okay, okay. I'll bet you a week's pay there's more traffic today about me missing the premiere than any of the Fashion Week stuff." He laughed. "No, if I win, you have to be nice for a week." Another laugh. "Nice as in pretending to be someone else. Anyone else."

Bree turned to leave. She needed to go, and she could only excuse eavesdropping for so long.

"Naomi, for God's sake, it's the numbers," he said, pushing himself over to another computer. "It's always been the numbers. It's me, remember? When have I ever had another motive? The minute the Bree thing stops paying off, we'll end it. There's nothing else going on, so you can stop with your concern. It's unnecessary."

A spike of ice went through Bree's body, ripping

her heart. None of it had mattered, the conversations she'd had with herself, her determination to be realistic, to focus on business. She'd been an idiot. A fool. The soul-sucking pain told her she'd fallen for him, waltzed right into an illusion, knowing it was an illusion, and she hadn't even realized the fantasy had taken over.

She backed away from the door as quietly as she could on trembling legs. It was weird; she could feel her pupils dilating, feel a chill that had nothing to do with the air around her. But shock was an absurd over-reaction, wasn't it? No matter what was going on in her head, she'd never *believed* Charlie loved her. She hadn't. That he'd liked her, yes. That they clicked? That last night had been mutually extraordinary?

Wrong. Wrong as wrong could be. She was a gim-mick. Nothing more. Nothing real. He'd told her up front, and she'd signed a legal document that confirmed it. None of this was Charlie's fault. Hell, she's the one who'd instigated the sex last night. She couldn't even blame him for that.

She had painted herself into this corner. And now that she was there, she had to get herself out. Now. She still had obligations, parties to attend as Charlie's date. He could walk out of his office any minute, and oh, God, if he suspected she had turned into one of *those women,* she'd die a thousand humiliated deaths.

It didn't hit her that she was in the living room until she saw the remains of their dinner on the coffee table. She needed to escape. Get her act together somewhere else. But she'd have to leave a note, something easy and quick.

There was the receipt from the Thai place. A pen in her purse. She scribbled "Thanks for the fun night. See you later!" It was all she could do not to run to the elevator, and even though it made no difference, she pushed the button over and over and over.

Finally, she flung herself into the small mirrored box, grasped the rail with both hands and held herself together. She would have to face the security people, the doorman, get a taxi.

Evidently, she'd learned a few things from Charlie. Like how to smile convincingly, and how to make idle conversation as if nothing whatsoever was wrong.

She even gave the cabdriver her address, and sat back for the ride.

Once she'd cleared Central Park West, she fell apart.

14

CHARLIE WAS ANGRY AFTER disconnecting from Naomi. He wasn't mad at her, not exactly, but she knew better than to keep pressing when he clearly didn't want to be pressed. That the woman kept his life together was an undisputed fact. He could probably survive her loss but even the idea bothered him. Nothing made him more aware of how important his routine was than the thought of his network splintering.

The inner circle—Naomi, the server techs that oversaw the equipment, his blog editors—were like his pulmonary system with Naomi at the heart. Which made it difficult to lie to her.

He'd done it before, mostly for the sake of ease. Trivial matters. That he'd missed the premiere, that he'd been with Bree over such an extended period of time, that he liked her, was not trivial at all.

He'd been staring at his monitor for several minutes without absorbing any data, but rather than getting back to business his eyes closed as the memory of Bree's body beneath him went straight from his brain to his cock.

She was probably still sleeping as it wasn't even eight, let alone eight-ish. The nice thing to do would be to leave her be. The girl was exhausted, and what they'd done last night hadn't helped. Yet he wanted to go to the bedroom right now and do it all over again. What the hell was up with that? They'd agreed, the sex might have been mind-blowing, but it wasn't smart. This was a rookie mistake, allowing his feelings into the mix. He'd end up as just another blogger if he wasn't careful. Someone who used to be someone.

He should wake her. Maybe with a cup of tea?

He pushed himself across the room, calling himself every kind of an idiot. Coffee was the polite thing to do. It was business as usual today. No screwing around. No goddamn tea.

This time, he'd give her a couple of twenties, make sure she took them. Explain to her how it was a write-off. That would get them both back on track.

She had work, they had the club opening tonight, and he had to put a spin on last night's premiere that would bump up the numbers.

As he went toward the kitchen to get her coffee, he saw her note. He picked it up, recognized her handwriting but didn't believe she'd left without saying anything to him. That she'd left a note instead. What the hell that wasn't like Bree. Had last night been that bad?

Shit, missing the premiere hadn't been like him. Maybe Naomi was right. Maybe he was too messed up to see clearly. He glanced down at her note and the rush of disappointment churning in his gut made him more determined than ever. Bree was a bit player in a long-running play, and he'd better start thinking of her only that way.

THERE WERE SIX OTHER people on her floor at work, which was six too many. Unfortunately she was no longer the invisible new girl. Now she was Charlie Winslow's date. The one whose byline was on the front page of *Naked New York*. She'd wanted to be noticed, and she'd gotten her wish. If she could have, she would have turned around and gone straight back home. But she couldn't put her job at risk. More at risk.

As she sank into her chair, Bree was incredibly grateful for the cubicle walls. She knew she looked like crap with her swollen eyes and her red blotchy skin, but who cared? What difference did it make, now that she understood? The awakening had been inevitable. At least she'd gotten some really good sex out of it, right?

No, she would not cry again. Instead, she took out the preliminary copy for one of their lesser accounts. She blinked back tears and yet one dropped on the word *latte* and the letters in the middle lost their definition, spread and blurred into something that looked like failure.

The copy had been terrible, anyway. She crushed the sheet of paper into a ball and tossed it into the trash bin under her desk. Naturally, she missed. The carpet was a dark, wavy blue that was meant to disguise, meant to trick the eye into thinking it was clean when it wasn't. She didn't bother picking up her mistake.

Her phone buzzed before she could turn to her keyboard. Rebecca, sending a text.

Call me. SOON!

Bree ignored it; the prospect of speaking to Rebecca made her queasy. It wasn't her friend's fault; it wasn't. She had done Bree an unbelievable favor. It was nobody's fault but her own. She'd read the rules, entered the game with her eyes wide-open.

The task of rewriting the copy was too much for her to bear and she considered leaving, going back to her hole-in-the-wall bedroom, cowering under the covers for a while, but couldn't. She'd file now, give herself time to calm down, stop thinking that her life was some kind of tragedy when it wasn't. God, she could be a drama queen.

Poor Bree, getting a chance to meet famous designers and go to all the best parties in New York. How horrible.

Her sigh made the top few pages of her filing stack flutter up like little skirts. She grabbed a handful of reports. Boring as hell, maintenance stuff like expenses, inventory and billable hours, but they had to be sorted before they could be shoved into files, and what happened to the mythical paperless office? They were probably right there next to flying cars and silver unitards for all.

The image of Charlie swooshing across his office in his fancy chair froze her. She blinked it away, but the image lingered, filling her chest with pressure.

The phone, again, and this time it was Lilly.

Can U meet 4 dinner? Or is CW taking U somewhere fab?

The expense reports went on the far corner of her desk, setting the border of the assembly line. There were seven distinct piles, and she put every ounce of her concentration on each item, neatly squaring each stack as she went, the tap tap of the paper against her desk loud in the gray cubicle with the calendar next to the picture of her parents and the clips from newspapers and magazines, all precisely placed with only blue pushpins that matched the carpet and looked good against the gray.

The phone. A text. Again. Only this one…

Hey, Bree. Member me? UR SISTER???? Pick UP. PICKUPPICKUPPICKUPPICKUP. Call me. Beth. Who misses you. Brat.

Bree squeezed her eyes shut so tight she saw stars, little flashes of white that should have been beautiful, should have been fireworks. The pressure in her chest had turned to homesickness so deep it was the Grand Canyon of ache, the Mariana Trench of despair. She wanted to be sitting at the little kitchen table, the one that was for breakfast if all the kids and grandkids weren't there.

She wanted her mother's biscuits with honey from the Iverson's bees, and she wanted thick cut pepper bacon and scrambled eggs, and to hear her father humming tunelessly as he prepared his plate.

She wanted the music that was playing so loud from Beth's room it would shake the rafters, and Willow to be barking like a fiend outside because the chickens weren't behaving, and she wanted to be little again. Safe. Filled with dreams that didn't have thorns.

When Charlie texted, she dropped the papers in her hands.

Missed you this am. Re: tonight. 7 ok? Dinner 1st. Tea? CW

She went to text back, got a blank screen, her thumbs at the ready. But she couldn't do it. All she had to say was okay. Nothing else. Because, of course, she was going to go. She'd signed an agreement. She had a responsibility. It was her *goddamned dream come true*.

She turned off her phone. Just for a while. Until she finished the filing.

CHARLIE TOOK A DRINK FROM the glass of scotch he'd taken from the party and wondered why he hadn't asked for a bottle instead. He looked over at Bree and gave her a smile even though she'd decided, as she'd done on the way to the party, to sit as far away from him as was possible.

In turn, she gave him a pathetic excuse for a smile.

What was going on? She'd texted him once all day, only to tell him she wouldn't be able to make it to dinner. He'd barely seen her as she was getting ready in the media room. He'd wanted to keep things focused, not mention the note or the night before. Her aloof attitude should have played right into his hand, but he hated it. He was still pissed about the stupid note. She could have said something even if they had made a mistake. He didn't like being caught off guard.

Once they'd entered the club, Bree had perked up, charmed everyone she'd spoken to. Had her picture taken, danced with men, women, groups of men. Not him, though. He didn't dance. Everyone knew that.

Of course, people had asked about missing the premiere, and he hadn't answered. Neither had she. The two of them had touched and even kissed, although on the cheek. They'd made sure the crowd believed what he wanted them to. The only fly in that ointment was that the touching and even that nothing kiss had made him hard in his suit, and he'd had to wait outside with the smokers until he'd calmed down.

Whatever the consequences, this bullshit couldn't go on. She wasn't tired; tired was different. Even through the smiles and the gossip and the pictures and the pounding noise she'd seemed dulled, muted. The spark that made her light up a room had been muffled, and that had happened sometime between the best sex of his whole life, and a note on the back of a take-out receipt. Each time he looked at her, he both wanted her, and wanted to know what had happened.

"You're quiet," he said finally, heading into the breach.

She did that thing with her mouth that was supposed to reassure him, but accomplished the opposite. "I worked so much longer than I'd planned, I barely got a nap, and then I woke up in a panic…"

He nodded, but he didn't believe her. "I'm sorry I've been keeping you out so late. We don't have anything going on tomorrow. That's a plus."

"It is," she said, staring at her hands.

"Bree. Did I do something I shouldn't have? I can be an insensitive bastard, I know."

She met his gaze squarely. "No. You did nothing wrong. Not at all. Not one thing. You've been exactly who you said you'd be, and that's great. That's…great."

"Great," he echoed quietly, because that little speech made his gut clench.

"Sorry. You know what? I got a call from home today. Family and stuff. With so little sleep, I suppose I'm not very good company."

For the first time since 8:00 a.m. Charlie relaxed. Not completely, but family crap he understood. God knows, every time he interacted with his family he snapped at everything for hours if not longer. "Anything I can do?"

She shook her head. "Thanks, but no. Nothing anyone

can do, but accept what is. I'll be fine by Monday. We've got that perfume party, right?"

He nodded. "Yeah. I don't even know how a celebrity begins to find a scent. I sure as hell don't remind myself of exotic spices or citrus fruit, for God's sake. And they make millions. Do people really think if they smell like someone supposedly smells, it makes them sexier? More likely to become a famous person themselves?"

Bree laughed—the best sound of the night. Even with the buzzing still in his ears. Finally, it felt right in the car, if a little cold. She was still very far away.

"You, on the other hand," he said, slipping closer to her, "would make a wonderful perfume."

She eyed him, and instead of touching her as he'd planned, he simply lowered his voice. "You smell like honey and the ocean. The nearer I get, the more pronounced it becomes. It's there no matter what, so either it's the best perfume ever, or as I suspect, it's just you."

"I don't wear perfume," she said. "And there's no honey in any cosmetic I own. I'm not even sure what the ocean smells like."

He shut his eyes as he inhaled. There it was. He was not making it up. "It's gorgeous," he said. "Like you."

Bree whimpered softly, which made him open his eyes, smile. But she wasn't looking at him. She was staring out the window. The feeling of everything being right again vanished.

"Bree—"

"I'm sorry. It's not you. I promise."

"Okay," he said, uncomfortable that he didn't know what to do here. "Would you like to come up?"

She stilled, barely even breathed and then shook her head. "Not tonight, but thank you for the offer."

He shifted slightly, giving her space. Then he picked up his half-empty glass planning to polish it off before they reached his building.

Bree threw caution to the wind when she ordered eggs 'n' apples Benedict on French toast with maple syrup. The others, Rebecca, Shannon and Lilly, gave her approving nods, and even a lift of a Mimosa, then ordered eggs or oatmeal. They were having Sunday brunch at Elephant & Castle, and Bree should have been starving after an hour's wait to get seated. Her hand trembled as she lifted her coffee cup.

"He was nice," Shannon said, and Bree smiled as Shannon flipped her red hair behind her shoulder. Shannon communicated with her body. Her eyes lit up with joy, her disappointment showed in her shoulders and the wry arch of her brow, and when she was angry she jutted her right hip and put her hand on her waist.

In Shannon-speak, the hair lift was more about inevitability than disappointment. A forgone conclusion. Bree didn't have enough hair to copy the move, nor the acceptance. Not yet.

"We should have clicked," Shannon continued, after polishing off her first cocktail. "God knows he was hot. I almost went home with him, but it seemed unfair. To his card, you know? He wants something long-term. Sadly, there were no sparks." She looked around the restaurant, the buzz of the place not intrusive but definitely there. "Is it really only biology? A chemistry project? That doesn't seem fair."

"Well," Lilly said, pulling a trading card from her bag. "Here's mine. No matter what, you'll enjoy the evening. He's a sweet guy, and extremely bright. Money, too."

Shannon took the card, and gave hers to Lilly. "Here's to you and John clicking like crazy."

They both studied their new prospects. Bree sipped her coffee and when her gaze shifted to Rebecca, the woman didn't even pretend she wasn't staring, had obviously been staring.

"What?" Bree said, petulantly enough that she hoped Rebecca would get it.

"What's going on?"

"Nothing. Everything's fine."

Rebecca picked up her Mimosa, but Bree heard her whisper, "liar," before she took a sip.

"Rebecca, please."

"If he's done something horrible, you have to tell me."

"He hasn't."

"Then—"

"It's nothing. I'm telling you. We're fine. We're going to a perfume party tomorrow night. I haven't slept in what feels like years, and I would be in bed now if you horrible people hadn't dragged me out."

"You've been AWOL for too long," Shannon said, "and all we know is what we read on the internet. I have fifty big ones riding on what you and Charlie Winslow were doing instead of attending that premiere."

Bree's face went up in flames, at least that was what it felt like. She traded her coffee for ice water, and willed herself pale. "Nothing of consequence," she said.

The three of them exchanged disbelieving glances and in one more second Bree was going to get her purse and walk out of the restaurant. Quit the lunch exchange group, never look at a trading card again and start checking out airfares to Ohio.

She flushed again, but not because of Shannon's comment. She might have made a mistake allowing her feelings to get out of hand with Charlie, but she was not going to leave the table, or the state. She was not that person, and dammit, it didn't matter how many tears she needed to shed until she got over her heartache, she would not give up. She hadn't come this far only to slink home to Mommy.

"Seriously," she said, sitting up straighter in her chair. "Nothing much happened. Our scheduling was off. Charlie parlayed it into gossip and it worked. We were a blind item in the *Post* today, Page Six. It's all part of the master plan. *NNY* lives for unique hits. It's a whole big mathematical formula that determines how much he can charge for ad space. All relative to individual times a certain person clicks on the blog on any individual computer."

"That's it?" Lilly asked skeptically. "But, you guys are so cute together."

Bree turned from Lilly to Rebecca, meeting their gazes. "We're supposed to look cute together. I'm sorry I'm spoiling it for you guys, but I swear, it's business. In fact, as soon as the numbers dip and I'm no longer useful to the blog, I'll be raiding the trading cards myself."

"You gonna throw Charlie back into the ring?" Shannon asked.

"Believe me. He's not your type. Oh, he's nice and all, but he's not looking to date."

Rebecca tried to stare her down, as if she could make Bree take it back with telepathy. Bree touched her hand. "We'll talk, but not now," she said, low enough that the others couldn't hear, and then there was the food, and that was the distraction she'd needed. She relaxed, confident she'd crossed an important milestone.

Then her phone rang. She almost ignored it. When she did take it out of her purse, she knew before she hit a single button that it was Charlie. Only it wasn't about tomorrow night's perfume extravaganza.

Dinner tonight? Chef's table at Le Bernardin?

Bree saw the name of the top-rated restaurant in the city. The invitation was more than incredible. For her career, for her future, she shouldn't hesitate. There would be pictures and even more gossip when they went out to dinner without an event chaser. But for her sanity, she typed:

Love to. Can't though. Other plans. See you tomorrow!

15

CHARLIE PICKED UP THE PHONE, a smile on his face before he heard the words from the security downstairs. When his cousin's name was announced he flicked an invitation to some bullshit party to the floor as he gave his assent.

Maybe Rebecca dropping by wasn't so bad. It was weird, but not necessarily a terrible thing. She was friends with Bree. Since she rarely visited, she had to be here because of that friendship. Rebecca would know what the deal was, and that would help. Or maybe she'd heard he was going to cancel his reservation at Le Bernardin and she wanted him to take her? Well tough, because he wasn't hungry anymore.

He got up from the dining room table, not bothering to pick up the invite or any of the other accumulated mess. His housekeeper would be back tomorrow. It wasn't until he opened his door that he realized he hadn't put on shoes. Just socks. Black socks. He was in his jeans, and his Yankees T-shirt. He'd laid out clothes for his seven o'clock date, but screw that.

Rebecca, as always, looked as polished as a cultured

pearl. He took her coat and tossed it over the ottoman by the entrance. Heard her indignant huff and ignored it.

"You want coffee? Wine? Vodka?"

"It's two-thirty in the afternoon," she said, her heels clicking behind him as she followed.

"And?"

"Can you even make coffee?"

"You're a riot, Becca."

In the kitchen, she got out the milk while he poured beans into his coffee mill.

When the grinding finished, he put the grounds into the coffeemaker, and stood in front of the counter, with his arms crossed. "So?"

"What have you done, Charlie?"

"About?"

"Don't be obtuse. To Bree."

"I haven't done anything. She's the one who's been…"

"Been what?"

He shrugged, turned to watch as the coffeemaker gurgled. "Quiet. Off. I don't know."

"Want to tell me why you guys missed the red carpet?"

"No."

"Fine. Coffee to go, then. Oh, and congratulations for remaining fourteen no matter how old you actually get. Excellent job. You must be so proud."

"What are you talking about?" He swung around again, in no mood.

"Okay, let's deal with first things first. Do you honestly believe your family needs to advertise in your blogs in order for Andrew to win this election?"

"Yes."

"Then your ego has officially gone off the charts. Their visit to you, Charles, was their version of an olive branch."

"As if I'd endorse that idiot?"

"They weren't asking for an endorsement. You take ad money from all sorts of lunatics. During the presidential campaign, you had both parties shouting each other down constantly. And I know you didn't vote for both."

"So you did set them up. Hell, I gave you more credit than was due."

"What?" she said, taking two steps toward him.

"You actually told them to approach me, didn't you?"

"No. I didn't. I heard about it ex post facto. From Uncle Ford."

"Christ. This family."

"Is your family." She touched his arm. "I don't know what's happened between you and Bree, honestly, but I know she's different. And you—you don't go to your blog correspondents. They come to you. You don't pretend to have a lover for this long. And you sure as heck don't worry if one of your gimmicks is quiet."

He stepped back, dislodging her hand. He took out two mugs and poured for them both. "It's not personal. The numbers are up. They have been since that first night. I suppose I should thank you for that."

"I don't give a damn about your numbers."

He sipped his coffee and it was so hot he scalded the top of his mouth. "That's all I care about."

"Yeah. Right." She got one of his now-famous to-go cups from the cupboard and transferred her coffee, adding some milk before she put on the top. "It's not going to be easy to go back. After Bree, it's going to hit you hard. At least, let's hope so. I think there's a decent man inside you, Charlie. I've known you too long to give up hope."

"Who died and made you Yoda?"

She grinned. "I can dish it out. Probably because I've all but turned into a monk. But you know what? If and when I find someone you think is worth fighting for, I give you my full permission to take no prisoners. You got that?" She stepped right up into his face and looked him in the eyes. "You fight for me, Charlie. Fight dirty. Fight hard. Don't let me be right when I need to be happy." She kissed him on the cheek, took her drink and left him standing in his socks.

By the time he remembered his own mug, it was cold. But he'd made a decision.

CHARLIE CALLED HER at one-ten on Monday. Bree picked up after the second ring.

"Charlie? What's wrong?"

"Nothing. Why?"

"You're not texting."

"Oh," he said. "No, everything's fine. How are you?"

"I'm great. Great."

He winced at that. Two *greats* definitely made something wrong. "Good. Because, you know, there's the perfume gig tonight."

"Right. I was going to text. What time did you want me at your place?"

He swung his chair around and stared out his window. The whole city seemed gray. Despondent. "Seven? Six if you want to eat. We won't be staying late. It's perfume. I promised a friend, or I'd cancel." Charlie waited for her to say something, and when the silence stretched, he had Plan B ready. "You, on the other hand, promised no one. Tonight isn't really a big deal. If you want to pass, that's fine."

"Pass?"

"Yeah. You've had a busy week, and Monday-night parties are always second tier. I'll make something of it in the blog, something that'll keep them talking. If you want."

The silence was broken by her breathing, and he tried to picture where she was. Indoors, as there was no sound of traffic. In her cubicle? A restaurant? He wondered if she had a ribbon in her hair today, and he wished he'd gone to talk to her in person. Her voice wasn't enough.

"That would be great," she said.

"Okay, then. No problem. Get some rest. Catch up on that sleep, because there are a some big doin's going on starting Tuesday." He grimaced, remembering that Tuesday afternoon he'd agreed to walk down the runway for charity, but that wasn't Bree's problem. She'd be at work.

"Okay," she said, in a very small voice. "I'll get some rest. I... Thank you, Charlie. But if you change your mind. If you think it would be better...for the blog for me to be there..."

"Nope. Got it covered. You can read all about it in tomorrow's *NNY.*"

She sighed. It sounded sad. He'd given her a lot of thought last night. Fine, he'd missed her. But there was no reason to think this mood was anything other than what she'd said, despite Rebecca's dramatics. Bree was far from home, on her own. She'd been slammed with brutal hours and tons of pressure. Tonight really was a lightweight affair, and while he'd rather be with Bree, he wanted her to take the time she needed to get herself back. He liked her happy. He liked her excited. He liked her.

IT WAS SIX-FIFTEEN ON MONDAY and Bree was in an elevator and it was possible that she'd actually lost her mind between the fifth and sixth floor.

Or maybe this trip was a direct result of not sleeping last night. She'd tried tea, yoga, meditation—that had been a laugh riot—a hot bath, warm milk. Instead of sleeping she'd read a year's worth of *Naked New York* blogs, every article she could find on Google about Charlie and every person he'd ever dated, started a new five-year plan a half-dozen times, and generally been insane. Work had been a circus. If she didn't get fired this week it would be because of divine intervention because she was not earning her salary. No matter what happened next, *that* was going to change. She would need BBDA more than ever after this ill-advised visit.

She hadn't called ahead. George at the front desk hadn't bothered to notify Charlie of her arrival, but he had asked if she'd been feeling okay because she hadn't been there on Sunday. George didn't work on Sunday. So he'd heard from other front desk personnel that she'd missed a night with Charlie. Which meant it wasn't just her—everyone thought Charlie and she were... something they weren't. She wasn't sure if that made her feel better or worse.

As the elevator approached his floor, she had to fight off utter panic because what was she even doing there? She had no idea what she was going to say. She honestly didn't want to go to the perfume party. Bree had never once imagined a world where that would be true.

Anyway, not going to the party felt worse. God help her, she missed him. Knowing everything she knew, she wanted him like an addict wanted crack. The break tonight was supposed to have been used for regaining her energy, refocusing on her goals, making that new five-year plan. Or sleep. Sleep would have been good.

The elevator stopped so smoothly it took her a second to get that she'd arrived. The second the doors whooshed open she panicked, pressed the down button. Twice.

As the doors were about to close, her arm shot out. And wasn't this just the picture of her life. Stuck. Unsure. Afraid to meet her own gaze in the mirror. Terrified to walk forward, unwilling to go back.

She had no plan, and that was the scariest thing of all. But she took those few steps out of the box, ready to face whatever had compelled her to come.

Charlie opened the front door before she knocked. When he saw her, his beautiful brown eyes widened and his smile was so brilliant and so genuine that something inside her changed forever. "Bree," he said with that damn voice of his.

"Hey."

"I thought—"

"I know. I wasn't—"

"Come in. The team isn't here, but we can do this. We can figure this out." He stepped back, his gaze and his smile steady and pleased. "I was just grabbing dinner. Pizza. Cheese and mushroom. I can get something else if you don't like pizza. There's that curry place I told you about—"

"I'm fine. It's fine. Pizza is great." They were standing inside. She was in her coat. Wearing a work dress, boots, nothing special, just clothes because she never imagined she'd get this far.

He was in jeans. A dark purple shirt with rolled-up sleeves. Socks, no shoes. His hair was messy, but not his usual cool messy. One important part was smooshed against his scalp and it made tears bubble and her throat tighten, which made no sense at all.

He came toward her, arms up, as she moved to shrug off her coat but then he hugged her, trapping her arms at her sides. Weird didn't come close to what was happening inside her. Tears on the edge of falling, a flurry of butterflies in her stomach, a blush of epic proportions and the smell of his skin both arousing and comforting.

She felt a little better when she caught him sniffing at her neck. Better still when the stiffness in his body and his stuttering breathing made it clear he felt as awkward as she did.

He stepped back, and oh, God, his blush. It was great. And awful. Because this wasn't what she wanted it to be. It *wasn't*. How could she not get that through her very thick skull?

She let her coat slide to the floor. It was all she could do not to follow it.

CHARLIE WATCHED HER WOBBLE, and he wasn't sure whether to grab her or what.

"Here's the thing," she said, her voice as shaky as her legs.

Charlie got caught by the pink of her cheeks and how she was trembling, and while she wore no ribbons, she did have a butterfly clip pulling back a small section of short, dark hair.

"I know not to mix things up." She tipped forward just a bit. "Business, pleasure. That kind of thing. I know that. You've been nothing but amazing, and you've completely changed my life. My five-year plan? It's fast-forwarded to two, maybe three now, but really, I'm rethinking the whole thing because I—it— I'm different. Because you let me write for you. You gave me carte blanche into the world I'd dreamed of, and dreams that come true become something else. Not bad, just not what I imagined. Which is okay."

She took a steadying breath, and man, she needed it because she'd pretty much said that all in one sentence.

Charlie understood her, though. Despite being swept up in her eyes, in her pink lips and how she flung her right hand to the side when she emphasized a word. He knew he was still smiling. Thought about stopping. Didn't.

"So the problem isn't you," she said. "It's that I broke the one rule. The big rule. The one that can ruin it all. I didn't know I was going to. I sure as hell didn't plan to. I'd made a promise. To myself. That I wouldn't get involved. I wouldn't let myself. Because my friends? My college roommate and all my BFFs from high school? Every one of them fell for a guy and then their dreams…diminished. And, yes, I know one doesn't have to lead to the other, but I know myself, and how I can be obsessive, and that's a great trait when I'm working toward my future, but not so great when it means I'm swallowed whole by love. It's not that I don't think love is good, 'cause it's fine—it's great—but my goals…they're important. I want to prove myself in the world before I settle down. Look at you! You went out and did exactly that. You haven't for a minute let anything or anyone get in your way, and wow, you've done it. You're the most successful man I know, and you didn't become a total sonofabitch doing it, and you have morals and you've been so nice to me, I don't even—"

Good God. Charlie blinked, and his smile cracked. Not completely, but enough. Love? Really? *Love?*

No. No, no, no. That wasn't what was happening here. He liked her. A lot. More than most people. A whole lot. Sex with her was off the charts, and as fantastic as that was, spending time with her was even better, but love?

Not happening. Not on the table. Not open for discussion, so what was she…

He was pretty sure a heart wasn't supposed to beat this fast.

"…but I think it's just because, you know, Cinderella and all," she said, her voice a little slower, her eyes not quite as vibrant. "Although I never expected that kind of happy ending. That's crazy talk. I mean, you're Charlie Winslow. You're the poster guy for living single. I'm the gimmick. Seriously, I know all that. It's fine with me. It's what I signed up for. I had it all planned out, see, how I was going to do this life, this part of my life, and then I went and did something stupid. Not that I'm exactly *in* love, but I'm heading there and if I'm not careful…" She swallowed. "It won't affect you at all. I mean that completely. If it makes you uncomfortable, well, then…"

She pressed her lips together for a second as a flash of hurt crossed her face. Or confusion? "Well, then, I'll just make myself scarce. That's cool. But if you still have the numbers, I'll live up to my agreement. I'll be the best damn gimmick I can be, and I won't embarrass you, I swear. I promise. It's my problem, not yours. Seriously. It's just that you've been so great, and I owed it to you to tell you what was really going on. You really have been great."

It was taking a long time for his brain to catch up to her words, and he might have missed a chunk in there somewhere. He thought she'd said she'd fallen in love? With him? Or maybe she was afraid of falling in love. With him. But she didn't want to because it was against the rules, and he was a poster child, and she was a gimmick. Or Cinderella.

He was pretty sure she'd mentioned it was her problem and not his, but there might be an argument in there about the veracity of that statement. If he gave it some thought, he'd be able to work it out, make sense of what she'd said, was still saying.

"You look terrified," she said. "I'm sorry. Don't be. I won't… I'm not… I'm not like a crazed fangirl or a stalker or anything like that."

She winced, and he'd seen that look before. It got to him, that scrunched-up face. Scrunched and beautiful, and oh, shit.

"Um," she said, softly. "That might have gotten away from me a little."

He had to clear his throat. "Bree, maybe we should go have a bite to eat. You know, slow down. Talk."

The knock on the door didn't register until Bree looked behind him. What the hell? Had the entire staff gone on vacation or something? "Just a sec," he said, then he went to the door.

It swung open and there was Mia Cavendish, in a massively huge faux fur coat, hair and makeup photo-ready and a look of such boredom on her face Charlie thought she might simply melt into a puddle in the atrium.

Mia glanced at Bree, then her wristwatch, then at Charlie. "Am I early? Naomi said to be here no later than six-thirty."

It was like being stabbed in the chest. Like an earthquake. Like a wake-up call. Bree tried to remember how to breathe as she prayed for the earth to swallow her whole, for the strength to move her damn feet before the elevator went back down to the lobby. She was *such* an *idiot*. And a liar, a total, complete liar.

"Naomi?" Charlie asked. "What?"

"For tonight's party," Mia said as she strode into his home as if she lived there. She smiled at Bree, although it was clear she couldn't be bothered. "I think this is what I'm going to wear, but I'm going to check the racks," she said, dropping her coat on an ottoman. "I'd kill for some champagne." She looked at Bree again. "Where's Anna? Oh, she's probably gone. Charlie?"

"Mia, when did you speak to Naomi?"

"This afternoon. Around one-thirty. Why?"

Bree heard them talking, but their voices were muffled. She needed to pick up her coat. Put it on. Get out. Now. Before Charlie noticed her again.

Although, why would he? One of the most beautiful women in the world was standing not five feet away. Tall, willowy, her face impossibly gorgeous—she was the kind of woman who should be with Charlie Winslow.

"Give us a minute, Mia. There's champagne in the fridge."

The model didn't look pleased about it, but she walked off, confident in her insanely high boots.

That got Bree moving. She bent at the knee, as her mother had taught her, to get her coat, and it was cold on her arms, heavy on her shoulders, but it was thick, and when she wrapped her arms around her waist it felt like protection. "I've got to go," she said, looking anywhere but at Charlie.

He came into her peripheral vision, and she stepped aside, quick as she could. "You know what's funny?" she asked while she backed up.

"Bree, wait."

"What's hysterical? I'm from Hicksville. That's the real town I'm from. Hicksville, Ohio. I went to Hicksville High, and nothing on earth has ever been more appropriate than that."

"What?" Charlie blinked at her, looked toward the kitchen, then back. "Wait, this is all going too fast. Don't go. Okay?"

She shook her head. "You've got to get ready. You made a promise, and you can't be skipping things. I've already knocked you out of your routine, and that's bad enough, but they're expecting you. And Mia Cavendish! That's going to raise some eyebrows, right? Wait till Page Six gets a load of you two together. Facebook is going to go nuts."

She hurried away from him, moving sideways, just as she'd done that first morning-after.

"Please," he said. "I don't—"

"It's okay. We'll decide what to do later. I really have to…" And she was out the door, hitting the damn elevator button, and why couldn't he have lived on the first floor? Would it have killed him? She would have been in a taxi already.

The elevator dinged, and she had never been so thankful. She stepped inside just as the door opened behind her, and Charlie walked out.

She found the close-now! button on the first try, and he didn't stick his arm out to stop the doors. Why should he? Charlie Winslow knew exactly where he belonged.

16

CHARLIE WANTED TO BE anywhere but at the Canal Room. The place was packed with the same people he'd seen Saturday night and Thursday night and Wednesday night. The same cameras and reporters and hangers-on made all the same noises. The play repeated endlessly and the only thing that changed was the costumes.

Mia was…somewhere. She'd seemed surprised when he hadn't cozied up after getting out of the car. It hadn't mattered that they'd not uttered a word during the drive, but when the cameras were rolling, there were expectations. Demands. He couldn't have cared less.

The press would say what they wanted to say, then it would be his move, and he'd make a more outrageous statement, and it would continue. Not even chess, but checkers. His thoughts, as he stood nursing a scotch near the rear exit, aside from debating making a run for it, were on the two women who had come to the center stage of his life. Rebecca, who had always been an ally, even when they'd been kids. There was no reason to believe, rationally, that she had changed her allegiance. He'd done nothing to hurt her or embarrass her. They weren't just relatives, they were friends.

Given that, perhaps it was time to consider what she'd been trying to tell him. She had nothing to gain by him reevaluating his relationship to his parents, to his business, to Bree. If he did a complete about-face in all three areas, he and Rebecca would continue on as before.

What was he afraid of? The idea of change? Change was always uncomfortable, and he'd made himself a very comfortable life. Say he was willing to step outside his patterns. Nothing written in stone, so what if he looked at it?

He was under no obligation to do anything his parents asked of him. He hadn't been for years. The life he led was his own. In return, nothing he did or said was going to influence his parents, unless they wanted to be influenced.

He sipped the scotch, felt the burn at the back of his throat. It occurred to him that the race had been over years ago, but Rebecca was right. He'd never stopped running. He'd been incredibly pleased with their horrified response to *Naked New York* and his notoriety. It represented everything they avoided like the plague: common interests, personal exposure, progressive views. Basically anything that wasn't them. He'd kept upping the stakes, they'd kept reacting with shock, with threats, with bribes. Huh. He'd made that little hamster wheel his life's work.

Why, of all the interesting things that were available to a man of his resources, was he still playing this ridiculous game? Movie stars? Fashion? Scandals? It wasn't that he thought all celebrity was nonsense—he didn't. Humans created celebrity culture because they were designed that way. There'd been gossip ever since there'd been speech. Technology only made it more immediate. It was part of the world, but only a tiny part, and when all was said and done, it wasn't a part he particularly valued, outside of the revenue it generated.

He took his glass with him and made his exit. He didn't have his coat, and dammit, it was freezing, but he wasn't willing to go back inside, not now.

He walked down the street, and even at twenty to eleven, there were people in the crosswalks, people talking, lights on, restaurants and bars filled to the rafters. God, he loved this city. The fantastic mess of it. Endlessly fascinating, and he was the luckiest son-ofabitch who lived there. Did he even know what to do with this world at his fingertips? If he walked away from *Naked New York* tomorrow, nothing significant would happen. He imagined he would still run the media group. That was fulfilling and he was damn proud of what he'd built. But if he never went to another party, never saw another premiere or opened another club, so what? Manhattan would find another king. He would have to figure out what he wanted to do with himself. His parents could stop being embarrassed by the women he went out with. Shit. He started laughing, out there on the sidewalk, and a couple walking behind him crossed the street in the middle of the road.

Oh, Rebecca was going to be unbearable. No one did smug like Rebecca. But what the hell. He owed her.

Not that he had decided to walk away. Not yet. It was too big a decision to make on a scotch and a confusing night. Besides, he had his team to think about. Transitions, changes, financial repercussions.

Which actually sounded like one hell of a good time.

Shivering, he circled back to the entrance to the club. He had no desire to go in, but he owed it to Mia to tell her she was on her own. So he braved the front door, ignored the strange looks at his reentry. Finding Mia was all he cared about at the moment. Because while leaving the spotlight of *NNY* was a big decision, it wasn't the most important one he needed to consider. Which brought him to the second woman.

If he was going to jump off the cliff without a safety net, he was pretty sure he didn't want to jump alone.

BREE WAS IN THE CLOSET. Her closet. On the ottoman mattress that pretended to be her bed. Her room might have been the size of a toaster oven, but it had a door and no one outside could hear her cry.

Although she wasn't crying at the moment. She was staring at her phone. She'd already decided she wouldn't be on the next plane to Ohio, but she wasn't back in Amazon warrior mode, either. She was sad. About as sad as a person who had so much could be.

That was the kicker. A full-on wallow wasn't possible, not when there were so many people with real problems. The only thing wrong with her life was that the boy didn't like her back. Not the end of the world, not unique, and who was to say Charlie was the great love of her life? Maybe he served a completely different purpose. What if her attraction to him was a test of her fortitude, her commitment to her future? Or a reminder that she had a functioning heart, and that she had to be far more careful with her emotions?

It could have nothing to do with love. He was a fairytale kind of guy, and she was human. She'd grown up on Disney movies and romantic notions. Charlie was magic. Of course she'd been swept away.

The problem was in pretending, fabricating, believing he'd been swept away, too.

She picked up her phone, clicked on Contacts and

went through her personal list. She liked Rebecca so much, but she was too close to the ache. Lilly was great, but they hadn't reached the heart-to-heart stage yet.

Bree was too embarrassed to call her Ohio crew. She'd felt so damn superior to them and their tragic mistakes. Talk about falling from the height of her own ego.

No, there was only one place to turn tonight, and that was family. Beth was two years older, and she'd been through a messy breakup before she'd found Max. She was also an amazing listener, and boy did Bree need to talk.

Beth answered after one ring. "Oh, thank God. I know something's wrong. Talk to me already, you insufferable brat."

Bree sniffed twice, and started from the beginning.

CHARLIE STARED INTO THE fireplace. It was late, or to be more accurate, early. He was dog-tired and he needed to sleep, but a lot had happened since he'd come home, and he was still reeling from it.

The moment he'd walked in, he'd headed for the office. The morning blog had been easy. He'd done the real work and built up the party and the fragrance—after all, they were spending big bucks to advertise the scent all over his blogs—and he'd kept the talk of Bree alive. It was surprisingly satisfying to call Mia an old friend. She'd hate that. Especially the old part. But she never stayed mad for long. Of course, he'd had to pump the next few days' worth of events, about the movers and shakers in Manhattan. Then he'd wrapped it up with something…personal.

With all that talk of Bree's goals and dreams, he'd gone back into his archives and reread his original business plan. It had been eye-opening. He'd come so damn far since those days, yet in some ways he'd hardly moved an inch. Right next to the archive file he'd kept copies of the scandal he'd created after being accepted into Harvard law to make sure his family would never consider him for anything of importance.

He'd purposefully gotten himself arrested for drugs. He'd planned it down to the last photograph—no one had been caught with drugs but him, and he'd made damn sure it was so circumstantial he'd never be taken to court. The damage was all in the gossip, in the inferences, in the pictures in the *Post* and the tabloids.

No matter how many attorneys tried to get his trust fund taken away, they hadn't been able to touch a penny.

Yeah. He could probably stop now. Give his folks and his whole family a break. Jesus, he could be an ass. On the other hand, he'd learned from the masters.

So, new plan. Bottom line? He was in a position where he could make a real difference in people's lives. He had money, access, some power. Politics was straight out. Not even a consideration. Creative problem solving? That held a lot of appeal, even if he wasn't sure what that would look like.

Bree by his side?

He stopped breathing as a picture formed, nothing noble or dramatic, just the two of them, lying in bed, in the dark. Naked. And yeah, okay, postcoital. But the fantasy was really about after. About talking. Soft talk in the middle of the night, about whatever. Touching her because he could, and her touching him back.

He thought about that last shot by Rebecca. The thing about fighting to be happy instead of right. Missing the premiere? That had been the easiest decision he'd made in ages. He could still feel the pleasure of having Bree sleeping against him, even with the tingling in his arms. He'd felt more relaxed, happier than he had any reason to be, and why? Not just because he'd put Bree first, but because he'd put himself first, too.

Holy...

Charlie turned away from the fireplace, and walked across the living room to the atrium, then into his office. His computer was still on. He never turned the damn thing off, so it was easy to sit back in his chair and pull up a blank screen.

As his fingers flew across the keyboard he found himself smiling. As the sky lightened over Manhattan, he got closer and closer to the cliff's edge, and there was no net in sight.

BREE HAD LEARNED A LOT in the past week about faking not only a smile, but an attitude, and she was putting her skills to the test as the doorman ushered her into Charlie's building.

"Nice to see you again, Ms. Kingston."

"Thank you, George." She nodded at the other staff in the lobby as she hurried to the elevator. She didn't really breathe until the doors had closed and she was alone. Pressing 18, her finger shook, which was unacceptable. This was business. Charlie already knew the worst about her, so tonight would be nothing but another party, another extraordinary opportunity to learn and network. That's what she'd told her sister, what she'd told herself over and over and over again.

Her shaking hand went back to the buttons and she pressed 17 in the nick of time. The elevator stopped with a whisper-soft bounce and Bree couldn't get out fast enough.

She stood in a hallway. Thank goodness. She hadn't even considered that other floors could be like Charlie's—private residences. No, this was a hall, although from where she stood she could only see two doors.

The carpet was incredibly thick, a rich aubergine, the walls a creamy yellow, and there were several wrought-iron plant stands along the wall with fantastic red gladiolus arrangements. Bree stared for a moment, not thinking about anything but how pretty and elegant it all looked and how in all her years she'd never imagined standing in a hallway like this one. Quiet, sophisticated, beyond classy. It made no sense. Nothing made sense anymore. Most of all the idea that Charlie Winslow could ever, ever want Bree Ellen Kingston, a daughter of Hicksville, Ohio, former member of 4-H, the Girl Scouts and the Aaron Carter fan club. It felt silly, ridiculous, that she'd entertained the notion for a single moment.

She pulled her cell out and clicked on the only text she'd received from Charlie all day.

6? CW

Her response had been the eloquent: K

She pulled up this morning's blog, Charlie's post about the perfume party. The bulk of it was just what it said on the box: who had been there, gossip, bands, more gossip. Barely a word about Mia Cavendish.

But the last paragraph…

Bree read the last paragraph again. Surely this time her heart wouldn't jump, her breath wouldn't catch.

The night could have been improved if the smokers had come inside, but that's nothing new. The upgrades at the Canal Room were minimal, but important. The men's room, the upstairs lounge and the new bartender were all worth a look. I imagine the ladies' bathroom was also better, but I have no confirmation. As for the reason for the party—Jazz and Cocktails perfume looks as sexy as the name, and it smells damn good. Not like the ocean and honey, but still, damn good.

The ocean and honey. God.

No. Nope, getting off at 17 hadn't worked. The hallway hadn't cured her; the moment of clarity hadn't been enough to make her see reason. She was still screwed. But she'd get through the night, because she wasn't thirteen. She'd put on her armor along with her makeup and she would be grateful and attentive and happy.

Okay, grateful and attentive.

She had to wait for the elevator and when she finally stepped inside it was empty. Which was good. She faced herself in the mirror. Back straight, eyes open and expressive, smile— careful, not too much. There. She was ready. Even the kick in the chest when she saw Charlie didn't knock her to her knees.

17

Seeing Bree step into the atrium stopped Charlie cold. He'd been saying something to Sveta, but he couldn't remember what. It didn't matter. "Hey," he said, holding out his hand to walk Bree into the house. "Rested?"

"Yeah," she said, although she glanced away when she spoke. "Thanks."

"I have some deli in the kitchen. You want to eat before you get ready?"

She made a beeline to the hallway that led to the media room. "No thanks. Not hungry."

Charlie followed, his mood on the downswing as he realized his master scheme for the evening was already going to hell. He could hear the team chattering away as they prepped the room, and he thought about the spread in the kitchen. He'd specifically gotten all the stuff Bree liked from the Carnegie Deli, including the Russian dressing and coleslaw for her corned beef sandwich.

Bree turned the corner, disappeared from view, and he staggered to a stop as it dawned on him that his "master scheme" to sweep Bree off her feet—a whole night that came complete with timetable, great mood lighting and a rather epic soundtrack—had left out only one thing. Bree herself.

Sveta swam in front of him, whipped her hair back in her usual dramatic style, then asked him three rapid-fire questions about tonight's book party.

He blinked at the woman and let her drag him down the hall to where the action was. As he entered the madhouse, he caught a glimpse of Bree in the big makeup mirror. She stared back and her gaze was so full of pain it nearly flattened him.

He'd realized last night that his decision to step away from the hands-on editing of his media group was a huge decision, but *this* leap he was about to make? It wasn't across a murmuring creek, it was across goddamn Niagara Falls. He'd sculpted himself a world that was made entirely of his rules, serving only himself, and every moment of every day was Charlie Winslow-shaped. The only thing he ever compromised on was the blog, but only when he had to, and only when it would serve the greater good—which was also all about his business, so no, he never really compromised at all.

It was good to be the king. And yet, how had he never noticed that it was also incredibly lonely?

Rebecca. She was good; he had to give her credit. She'd said this would happen. That being right only went so far. He wanted more now. More with Bree. With the woman sitting in the center of a whirlwind.

But could he do it? Could he change in the ways he'd need to, to actually be part of a couple? Put her first? A novel concept, and one he'd botched at the starting gate.

He'd been so caught up in the grand gesture that he'd

forgotten that he was about to ask a great deal of this woman. She had her own dreams, her own goals, her wondrous five-year plan. Would she even want what he was proposing? Maybe he should wait, think this through. Acting rashly wasn't in his nature. This was crazy.

He refocused on Bree. She hadn't turned away at all. But she'd done a very good job of masking her pain. Anyone else would have thought that smile was real, that her eyes were bright with excitement and anticipation. But he'd seen her when she was truly happy.

The hell with it. He was going in. "Can I have everyone's attention?"

It didn't take long for the group to settle. "Something's come up. We won't be going to tonight's event, so, if you guys could wrap up what you need to, that would be appreciated."

He knew the whole team would react, but his gaze stayed on Bree's image in the mirror. She looked completely confused, but he wouldn't keep her there long.

"Don't worry," he whispered, then cleared his throat and spoke to the team again. "Don't worry, you'll all get paid for the night's work. There's food in the kitchen. Take it with you. I'll never be able to finish it. Thank you, everyone. Sorry for the inconvenience."

Sveta barely blinked. She started putting the clothes back on the racks, boxing shoes, making sure everything would be in order for the next event. The team followed suit, and since they'd only begun it was a matter of minutes before they were clearing out.

Bree rose from the makeup chair. She grabbed her pocketbook, tugged the bottom of her very-Bree vintage sailor dress. God, she looked sweet. He couldn't help the ache that went from his chest on down. He wanted her to say yes as badly as he'd wanted anything in his life.

Charlie was aware that the team members were staring at him, at Bree, and that they were trying to clear out as quickly as they could. He didn't care.

Bree had her head bowed but her spine straight and tall as she followed the small group. At the door, he caught her hand in his. "I'd like you to stay," he said. "Please."

When they were alone, and they could no longer hear the footfalls of the others, she met his gaze. "What's going on?"

"I had it all planned out," he said. "Like I was writing a play. We'd go to the party, but we wouldn't stay late. I'd convince you to come back here with me. I had a couple of backup plans for that, just in case. It would have been great. Very dramatic." He stared at her, at those amazing green eyes. "But all that really matters right now is how very much I want to kiss you."

"We're not going to the book party because you want to kiss me?"

He smiled. "No," he said, then half winced. "Sort of."

"Oh," she said, as if everything made sense. A second later she shook her head. "I don't get this at all. Charlie, what—"

He kissed her. He couldn't wait another second. Honestly, he didn't want to keep her in suspense—that wouldn't be fair. As soon as he finished this kiss, he'd tell her everything.

Then she kissed him back.

His first response was *thank God*. This was what he'd needed. Bree in his arms, on his lips. The taste of her minty gum and the slide of her tongue made him ache.

"Charlie," she whispered, and it was like a match to kindling, the sound of his name on her lips. He stepped into her. He would have climbed inside her if he could have; instead he walked her back until he had pressed her against the wall, kissing her as if his life depended on it.

With a gasp, her head thunked back, her mouth swollen and damp and irresistible.

He forced himself to slow down. The first brush of his lips was soft, gentle. Tender. But it wasn't enough, and he hauled her up against him, his mouth hard, hungry, desperate, as the kiss deepened into an intense tangle of tongues and teeth that made him groan.

Tearing her mouth free, she gasped for breath as her small hands got busy on the buttons of his shirt. Her eyes were wide and wild as she fumbled and cursed.

"Bree—"

She gave up on his buttons and went for his belt. He groaned, but no.

"Not here," he said roughly, and wrapped his arms tight around her, lifting her straight up, bending slightly until she wrapped her legs above his hips. He wanted to just get them to the bedroom, but as always, he couldn't resist kissing her over and over. He swerved like a drunk, dizzy with the feel of her, with the promise of what was to come.

Somehow, they made it to his room and they stripped. No finesse, no teasing. Simply the need to be naked. Now. As they stretched out on the bed, he took her hands in his and guided them above her head as he balanced himself over her body. He looked down into her face and saw a new life.

THERE WAS SO MUCH IN HIS gaze that Bree went still. She was a lost cause, gone, any good sense she had swept away by passion and the awareness of his body. When he whispered her name, the world slowed, the air thrummed with heat and want.

His mouth spread hot, wet kisses down her jaw, along her collarbone. Her breast. His tongue curled around her nipple and he groaned when it beaded for him.

She bucked, and he did it again, reaching for the drawer, grabbing a condom. He protected them both with fingers that actually trembled, and then nestled between her legs. The moon bathed them in soft gray light, so luminous it was enough for her to see the details of his face, although she already knew each feature intimately, and could have sculpted each curve.

"Missed you," he whispered, but his words turned into a moan when he sank into her.

Her eyes closed as he filled her, and her pulse quickened when she pushed up to meet his slow thrust.

They stilled when he could go no farther, their panting breaths loud in the room, but soon it wasn't enough and she pushed up again.

"Move," she said, squeezing his arms, pressing her breasts into his chest.

"God, yes," he said, so softly she barely heard him past the pulse of her heartbeat.

"So good." He cupped her face as he pulled out

slowly, kissing her after a languid swipe of his tongue across her bottom lip.

Her breath stuttered with the shock of his tenderness. She'd been ready for frantic sex. Not this.

He slid his hands to her hips and rocked, going even deeper now, and thinking was all but impossible. Tossing back her head, she gasped his name, and he thrust as if each time would be his last. Again and again, his control driving her wild. She could hear her own heart thundering in her ears, their mingled murmurs and cries, raggedy gasps and low moans. Hers and his.

When his fingers slipped between them, he barely had to touch her. A long moment stretched like a tightrope in that unbearably sweet limbo just before the crash, and when it came, when her orgasm tore through her like a bolt of lightning, she cried out and clung to him as if he was the only real thing.

He didn't let her go, and he didn't stop. Between her trembling spasms he said her name again and again, and as the pace increased his voice got louder until he filled her so completely she felt him come from the inside.

Finally, he fell beside her, close, and she felt small and tender against his damp body as her gasps slowed. When thought returned as a trickle, everything was perfect and peaceful and nothing else. But the trickle turned into a stream and that brought panic along with clarity.

Oh, God, she'd done it now. Again. She'd made things a million times worse. She should have left while she could have, made a break for it and kept on running. Because they'd made love. The sound of her name in his low voice was imprinted forever. She was a goner.

She rolled away from him and out of the bed, grabbing her dress from the floor. If she was lucky, she could still make a quick getaway and salvage some part of her heart.

His hand on her wrist stopped her.

"I have to go," she said, her voice quivering and her heart pounding.

"No, please. Wait." He tugged. "Please."

She took in a big breath before she faced him. "I appreciate all you've done for me, Charlie, but this was a mistake. You and I both know it. I can't kid myself anymore. Not after this. I have to stop. Full stop. No working parties with you, no writing sidebars, nothing. I've stepped over the line and there's no road back except the one that takes me far away from you."

He sat up, never releasing her wrist. "Bree, please. I promise I won't stop you if you still feel this way after... Ten minutes. That's all I'm asking."

Bree's dress wasn't on, in fact, it just hung from her hand and for a moment she stared at it as if it was something she'd never seen before, but it wasn't her dress that had her blinking. Things were getting mixed-up again, and she was already so far past the line with Charlie she'd lost all her ground rules. There was no getting around it. She had fallen in love with him. Nothing would fix that except time and distance. But ten minutes? She could risk that, right? But only if she wasn't naked.

He let go of her, and then she slipped her dress on. Her panties were puddled by the door, but she could get those in a minute. Now, though, she needed to hear what he had to say.

She sat down on the bed, not close, either. If he touched her, there was a very good chance the tiny bit of backbone she'd found would vanish like smoke. "I'm listening."

He nodded, but then did some maneuvering under the sheet that had become a bundle at the foot of the bed. He dragged out his boxer briefs snagged by his toes, and he smiled with the achievement as he slipped them on.

That little grin didn't help. It was clear that ten minutes was nine minutes and fifty-nine seconds too long. She should have run when she had the chance.

NOW THAT CHARLIE WAS really going to tell Bree about the plan, there was more than a hint of panic involved. He sat up, bolstered his back with a hastily arranged pillow, then met her gaze. Might as well just dive into the deep end. "Okay. First, I need to ask you a question. Did you have a good time Friday night? When we missed the premiere?"

Still looking a little dumbstruck, she nodded. "Yeah. Yeah, I did."

"Were you happy?"

A flash of pain was there and gone in a breath. "Yes. Very."

"Me, too."

Bree looked at him as if he was nuts, and he supposed she was right.

"I was really happy that night," he said. "I didn't give a damn about the red carpet or the blog. I wanted to be exactly where I was. With you. I didn't expect that."

"That's..." She floundered for a moment, her hands rising, falling into her lap. "Amazing."

"You can say that again. I haven't felt this way about anyone, not for ages—actually, never. I like you so damn much." It was horrible not to touch her.

Wrong. He abandoned his pillow and swung his legs over, scooting inelegantly until they were sitting side by side, touching. Until he had her hand in his. "I haven't wanted to talk with anyone the way I want to talk with you. Going to parties this week has been a revelation. And working together, well, damn that's been…"

He lost his train of thought as she blinked up at him, her mouth open in what looked more like shock than confusion. Yet when she straightened her shoulders and leaned away from him, he was the one who was confused.

"I'm glad," she said. "I am. And maybe in a while I can come back on board, because what you've given me… But I have to focus on my goals. Especially now that they've changed. I'm not even sure what exactly I want, but I know it's important to keep my eye on the prize, and not let myself get distracted. And sorry, Charlie, but you're the biggest distraction ever."

"No, no. Wait, Bree. Don't decide yet. 'Cause I'm talking about change, too. For the better, I hope. Look, the last thing on earth I'd ever want is to sideline your dreams. I believe in you. You're a talented writer, and you have an eye for detail and fashion. You'll be successful no matter what you decide you want to do, and a big part of what I want to do is support you in any way I can."

She exhaled a big breath. "Okay…"

"I've decided to step down as editor of *NNY*."

"What?"

He grinned at how loudly the word echoed in the moonlit bedroom. "It's time to take on some new challenges. That don't involve celebrities or supermodels or fashion shows. I have no idea what that'll look like. Just that it won't be what it has been."

"Oh," she said again, and he could practically see her mind struggling to make sense of what he was telling her, rearranging everything she knew about him. Hell, throwing it all out the window.

He brushed her cheek with the tips of his fingers. He wanted her to say yes so badly. "We're good together. We are. We fit. I want to explore that. Together. While we both find out where we belong individually. Because I'm pretty sure I'm in love with you."

BREE THOUGHT ABOUT pinching herself. But when she looked at his eyes she believed him. He loved her.

"Oh, my goodness," she said.

He laughed. "Yeah."

"You love me? Me?"

Charlie nodded. "Not sure I'll be any good at it. You know, first time and all."

She swallowed as she struggled to appear as if she wasn't freaking out. "That's okay. You're pretty good at everything else. I imagine you'll pick it up quickly."

"Thanks," he said.

It was her turn to touch, to run her hand up his arm before she caressed his cheek. That helped a lot. She'd needed grounding and the feel of him was familiar and lovely. "Are you sure about this? Really sure?"

"Oh, yeah. I'm in."

"This is insane. This isn't even a life I could have imagined, and when I was seven I wanted to be a unicorn."

He laughed as he pulled her close, as his lips captured hers and she could taste his grin and his excitement. She was ten feet off the ground, in the arms of the soon-to-be-abdicating King of Manhattan, and the hell with a unicorn. She was Bree, and she wouldn't trade that for the world.

She thought about her friends at the St. Marks lunch exchange, and how they were all so hopeful and scared when they picked up a trading card. She couldn't wait to tell them not to give up. Ever. Anything was possible. Anything.

The Next Day...

Huffpost Entertainment: CHARLIE WINSLOW QUITS!

New York Post: Today in Page Six...No More *Naked New York?*

FACEBOOK

| edit profile |

Charlie Winslow
Editor in Chief/CEO *Naked New York Media Group*
Studied Business/Marketing at *Harvard University*
Lives in *Manhattan* ❤ In a Relationship

* * * * *

PASSION

For a spicier, decidedly hotter read—
this is your destination for romance!

Harlequin® Blaze

COMING NEXT MONTH
AVAILABLE FEBRUARY 28, 2012

#669 TIME OUT
Jill Shalvis

#670 ONCE A HERO...
Uniformly Hot!
Jillian Burns

#671 HAVE ME
It's Trading Men!
Jo Leigh

#672 TAKE IT DOWN
Island Nights
Kira Sinclair

#673 BLAME IT ON THE BACHELOR
All the Groom's Men
Karen Kendall

#674 THE PLAYER'S CLUB: FINN
The Player's Club
Cathy Yardley

REQUEST YOUR FREE BOOKS!
2 FREE NOVELS PLUS 2 FREE GIFTS!

❦Harlequin *Blaze*™

red-hot reads!

New York Times *and* USA TODAY *bestselling author*
Maya Banks presents book three in her miniseries
PREGNANCY & PASSION.

TEMPTED BY HER INNOCENT KISS

Available March 2012 from Harlequin Desire!

There came a time in a man's life when he knew he was
well and truly caught. Devon Carter stared down at the diamond ring nestled in velvet and acknowledged that this was
one such time. He snapped the lid closed and shoved the
box into the breast pocket of his suit.

He had two choices. He could marry Ashley Copeland
and fulfill his goal of merging his company with Copeland
Hotels, thus creating the largest, most exclusive line of re-
sorts in the world, or he could refuse and lose it all.

Put in that light, there wasn't much he could do except
pop the question.

The doorman to his Manhattan high-rise apartment hurried to open the door as Devon strode toward the street.
He took a deep breath before ducking into his car, and the
driver pulled into traffic.

Tonight was the night. All of his careful wooing, the
countless dinners, kisses that started brief and casual and
became more breathless —all a lead-up to tonight. Tonight
his seduction of Ashley Copeland would be complete, and
then he'd ask her to marry him.

He shook his head as the absurdity of the situation hit
him for the hundredth time. Personally, he thought William
Copeland was crazy for forcing his daughter down Devon's
throat.

Ashley was a sweet enough girl, but Devon had no desire

to marry anyone.

William had other plans. He'd told Devon that Ashley had no head for the family business. She was too softhearted, too naive. So he'd made Ashley part of the deal. The catch? Ashley wasn't to know of it. Which meant Devon was stuck playing stupid games.

Ashley was supposed to think this was a grand love match. She was a starry-eyed woman who preferred her animal-rescue foundation over board meetings, charts and financials for Copeland Hotels.

If she ever found out the truth, she wouldn't take it well.

And hell, he couldn't blame her.

But no matter the reason for his proposal, before the night was over, she'd have no doubts that she belonged to him.

What will happen when Devon marries Ashley?
Find out in Maya Banks's passionate new novel
TEMPTED BY HER INNOCENT KISS
Available March 2012 from Harlequin Desire!

USA TODAY bestselling author

Carol Marinelli

begins a daring duet.

THE SECRETS *of* XANOS

*Two brothers alike in charisma and power;
separated at birth and seeking revenge…*

Nico has always felt like an outsider. He's turned his back on his
parents' fortune to become one of Xanos's most powerful exports
and nothing will stand in his way—until he stumbles
upon a virgin bride….

Zander took his chances on the streets rather than spending another
moment under his cruel father's roof. Now he is unrivaled in
business—and the bedroom! He wants the best people around him,
and Charlotte is the best PA! Can he tempt her
over to the dark side…?

A SHAMEFUL CONSEQUENCE
Available in March

AN INDECENT PROPOSITION
Available in April

better, but love?